I0761684

TANGERINN

Emanuela Anechoum

TANGERINN

Translated from the Italian
by Lucy Rand

Europa Editions
27 Union Square West, Suite 302
New York NY 10003
www.europaeditions.com
info@europaeditions.com

First publication 2026 by Europa Editions
Second printing, 2026

Translation by Lucy Rand
Original title: *Tangerinn*

At page 247, *Historiae* by Antonella Anedda.
Translated by Patrizio Ceccagnoli and Susan Stewart.
New York: New York Review Books, 2023.

Library of Congress Cataloging in Publication Data is available
ISBN 979-8-88966-160-3

Anechoum, Emanuela
Tangerinn

Cover design and illustration by Ginevra Rapisardi

Prepress by Grafica Punto Print – Rome

Printed in Canada

CONTENTS

Men like you, who have two different kinds of blood in their veins, never find peace or happiness: when they're there, they want to be here, and as soon as they return here immediately want to flee. You'll go from one place to another, as if you'd escaped from prison, or were in pursuit of someone; but in reality you'll only be following the diverse fates that are mixed in your blood, because your blood is like a hybrid animal, a griffin, or a mermaid.

—ELSA MORANTE, *Arturo's Island,*
translated by Ann Goldstein

TANGERINN

Between 1923 and 1956 Tangier, Morocco, was governed by an international commission made up of various European states. The city enjoyed political and military neutrality, freedom of trade, and a relative elasticity in terms of how people lived. It was defined as an International Zone, a no-man's land, which leant it a bohemian tolerance that over the years attracted a significant number of artists and poets, including William Burroughs, Jack Kerouac, Allen Ginsberg, and Paul Bowles. Next to the famous Hotel El-Muniria, where the beatniks liked to stay when they were in town, there was a small but welcoming bar called The Tangerinn. That was where they hung out, and it still bears many traces of that era.

You will find a glossary of Arabic words and phrases at the end of the book.

Prologue

You always ended up with the winning hand. You struggled, you were hungry, you had worked every day since you were this tall, you'd tell me. But the important things, the truly important things, just seemed to fall out of the sky. You had talent, but you would've been fine without.

Some of these things bear naming, while others, if said aloud, would feel like a betrayal. Most are not things you pursued, built, or designed yourself. They just happened to you, quirks of fate. Did you deserve them?

Playing cards with Samir down at the neighborhood bar. It didn't have a name, the sign just said *Café* in French. You played every day, yet there was always a hint of adrenaline, a pressure to win as if your life depended on it. It was a drug, always treading the line between strategy and luck. You had to prove you were good enough, because if not, what was Allah's plan for keeping you alive when your father and two of your brothers were dead?

Your first memory: you were three, your mother silently dabbed at her eyes while holding a tiny lifeless body in her arms. You ran down the stairs—you lived on the first floor of a two-story building—and out into the street to call the imam. They prayed and cried, cried and prayed, for days. The neighbors brought baskets of flowers and cinnamon to mask the stench, because the little body was changing color and starting to smell. Then they took it away. A few weeks later you started Qur'an school. Learning to pray was learning to write, to sing, to live. You didn't think about the dead, but every so often the image of that body came into your mind, and you feared he was watching you sleep. You were alive and he wasn't.

Everyone in the neighborhood understood. For some, faith was resignation, for others it was comfort; for you it was fatalism. Allah had to have a plan for your life. And when it was revealed, you needed to be ready. Samir also thought like that. He was different from you in so many ways, but he understood that winning was important, even if it was only at cards. That's why you were friends. Years later, in your other life, the one where I existed too, I watched you sitting on the carpet in the living room creating complex games of solitaire with playing cards. You had to win. You had to win even against yourself.

You didn't know what Allah had in store for you, but you hoped it would involve you both. You whispered your most secret plans to one another. One day you would drive to Tangier and board a boat. You would become rich, you'd live in Europe. One day you would both have beautiful wives, call taxis from hotel lobbies and fly on airplanes. You'd pay with a credit card, one of the gold ones. You'd never be hungry. You'd come back to the neighborhood as weary travelers, each time more foreign to your surroundings, with your branded trainers, shirts, the luminous skin of men who didn't work too hard. But your eyes would fall on the dusty unpaved roads with a nostalgia you didn't expect.

There are things that bear naming. Like jidda's hands, knobby and ancient like the roots of an olive tree. You'd kiss them on the palms and backs every time you entered her room. They smelled of spices and henna. Her nails were broken from scrubbing sheets and working fabric. She would sit bent over the sewing machine for as long as it took, never taking a break, slow and dedicated like prayer. Sometimes she sang as she worked, in a low and raspy voice. When she was tired, she would lean back into her chair and place her palms on the table. She'd stay like that for a few minutes, then return to work. Her small hands were always warm, you could squeeze them both in one of your own. You had big hands with long fingers and flat nails like a strange animal; clumsy hands that couldn't hold a flower. As a child I'd curl up in them and fall asleep. Your hands were the only home in which I've ever felt safe.

Ammi Boubakar's smile. He was kind of crazy: he believed in spirits, heard sounds that other people didn't, could see your dead brothers and sometimes spoke to cats. He was afraid of the dark. He was sad when the leaves fell from the trees, because they were dead and he hadn't got to know them in time. After the rain he went out to pick up snails from the road and, if he saw one that had been crushed, he'd cry. He was like a child in an adult's body. Innocent. When you left, he rode his bike to the port with you, saw you off without a word, not even a hug, but you knew he'd turned away to hide his tears.

Other things that need naming: Idris's Walkman, the way Zahra rubbed her swollen belly, the smell in the bar of mint and hashish, the running shoes Malik bought you with his first paycheck, jidda's hands—did I already say that?—and the price of flour, the hunger, the sounds of Derb Sultan, the flabby bodies of the old people in the fog of the hammam, skin wrinkly from the steam, from time, the blinding, bewildering colors of the market, women distractedly adjusting their hijabs, walking, chatting, and you following them with your eyes, like ghosts. As a boy, with jidda, you used to be scared you'd get lost and she wouldn't look back to find you, lost one son lost them all, the dogs that nearly took your leg off, the time you tried to steal apples from the neighbor's garden, the guy that sold odd shoes on the street corner, for people who only had one foot, the witches that read your tea leaves, the howling of the wolves in the distance from one of your great aunts' houses at the edge of the desert, lying on the roof with the stars so close it felt like they were falling down, the frightening sound of the waves in Melilla, when the current pulled you out and you were afraid of dying, when you ran from the police and you were afraid of dying, when you woke in the middle of the night and you were afraid of dying, there was a bullet hole in the living room window, you watched it, Boubakar grumbled in his sleep. A tear, like ripped fabric, but inside, beneath your sternum. It made you feel like you were and weren't there, in that moment when you dreamed of elsewhere. A restlessness, like a spirit, which lay on your chest at night as you thought of the day you would leave, as you thought about how life would be away from home—that you would call home another place, another bed, other walls. You wanted it, you wanted it, you wanted it, you told yourself, I told myself, because you were—you had to be—special to exist.

It was hard to breathe in those moments, and we were afraid of dying.

Part One

1.

When Berta called, I was with Liz at The French House, a small pub in Soho with bohemian décor. The little round tables felt Parisian and the walls were papered with photos of famous and not-so-famous writers and artists who had drunk there fifty or a hundred years ago. A glass of red wine cost eight pounds. They didn't sell crisps. The bartenders all had the same hairstyle, a bowl cut with a short fringe. The clientele was intellectual because they preferred wine to beer, talked fast and drank slow: acts of continental dissent. I once tried to get an interview thinking that, because they had parquet, being a barmaid there would've automatically made me less of a loser than being a barmaid somewhere else. They told me I didn't look French enough, but what they probably meant was that I looked too Italian, or too Arab. Neither was to the tastes of the French.

While you were dying, I was pretending to choose what to order. In reality, I always chose the cheapest thing on the menu, but in front of Liz I hesitated, as if weighing up the options. I thought constantly about how I looked to others, and in that moment I was probably thinking about how good my life must look from outside.

You died on a random day and, like on any other random day, I wasn't there. Between us there were two thousand kilometers and all the things left unsaid.

That afternoon Liz had sat down without taking off her

hat—a blue velvet fedora, worn without irony—and announced that a word had been removed from our vocabulary. I say "our" because she was helping me learn English and, as my tutor, she took the liberty of adding and removing words to my vocabulary according to what she felt needed to take priority.

What word? I asked, and I felt nervous, because all the words I knew had been hard-earned.

Envy. It's a toxic emotion, don't you think? You can't imagine how many people write to me saying they envy my body, my fashion taste, my money, my life. And they almost always go on to insult me. Every person who envies me ends up calling me a whore. What do they know about me? What kind of person are you if you don't want others to have what you want for yourself? It's immoral. If you look at other people in the way you should look at yourself it means you have some kind of deep hole inside you. I can't, it's just too sad, she concluded, and took a sip of wine, her blue eyes studying my reaction through the glass. At home she had a hidden stash of cheap Chardonnay which she drank with ice cubes.

Liz identified as a digital activist: that was her job. Every day, she received all kinds of products, from food to books, which she would review on YouTube and Instagram. She talked a lot about feminism, which meant she publicized things like graphic novels about Frida Kahlo and vegan soap. Her feminism was intersectional—obviously—but away from the camera Liz only spent time with other white women. I was an exception, but Arabs are considered practically Caucasian anyway, so I'm only just mixed-race.

Among the first things Liz taught me about feminism was that you must never make other women pay the price of your freedom; it's men who need to look after that. She considered herself too modern to worry about domestic chores, but she hated untidiness, dust, and neglect, so she hired men to come and clean the house. To avoid having to interact with them, she selected them from an app and arranged it so she would never be home when they came.

She had a t-shirt with Bernie Sanders' face on which she'd bought on Etsy, which wasn't like Amazon. She didn't like waste, so used solid shampoo bars from Lush, but if she was undecided between two tops she would just buy them both. At any rate, she'd say, they last me, like, forever, because I look after things so well. Meaning that she did the laundry with maniacal precision, separating by shade of color and washing just two or three items at a time with a huge quantity of fabric softener. She believed in Whole Foods, but also in shopping at the farmer's market. I couldn't afford either and felt guilty, because at Tesco they use so much plastic and you don't know who picked your bananas. She told me that sometimes making ethical choices was a privilege and rubbed my shoulder in absolution.

I felt a weight on my chest, a knot in my throat. I thought: I envy everyone, all the time. I constantly envy people who are beautiful, rich, happy, sure of themselves. I'm full of venom for other people's privilege, and I also envy their merits. I hope Liz loses everything she has.

That was when the phone rang.

I'm on the tube, can I call you back?

Mina—Berta's sobs didn't give me any kind of clue. It could have been anything or it could have been the worst thing.

It was the worst thing.

2.

Six years earlier I had knocked on Liz's door after seeing an ad for a single room in a two-bedroom flat looking out onto a quaint garden. I was twenty and I wanted to forget myself as quickly as I could. I was sleeping in a hostel, in a mixed dorm, and I wasn't used to the smell of men. Everything scared me, but I forced myself to face up to the new reality that I had chosen: a game of balance between longing to be seen and being terrified of it.

In fabricating the new me, the first thing I needed to find was the set: the place I would come home to each night. I had a clear idea of how it should look. A Victorian house, in a little street of clean, tidy, identical terraced houses. I found comfort in predictable architecture. The interior was important too, and there needed to be a certain atmosphere: a mysterious lamp with tassels, a dark velvet armchair, a Persian rug brought back from a holiday or from one of those second-hand markets where, I imagined, the new me would spend hours rummaging through old trinkets. On the walls there would be brightly-colored artwork that would draw a certain kind of gaze. A blocked-in fireplace and on its mantelpiece some books of poetry that I would pretend to read on Sunday mornings when, in reality, the half-open book would lie upturned on the table like a dead animal while I scrolled through Instagram instead. I wanted to feel surrounded by inconsequential beauty, which would protect me from the eyes of others.

* * *

Liz's house was near Canonbury station, an area inhabited mostly by Turks and other young people from southern Europe who had jobs as waiters and a passion for shakshuka. A couple of tube stops away was Hackney, the city's hip neighborhood, where people who didn't have the guts to actually live there went on the weekends and pretended to be woke. It was a well-loved activity in this city, the practice of brushing shoulders with those less privileged, to feel illumined, involved, but not having to make too much effort: to be in proximity to untidy, complicated, miserable lives.

A few years later the area would be invaded by people who were nearly thirty and recently made managers. Those who'd had the money to buy their own council houses, once reserved for people who couldn't afford rent, would sell them for half a million pounds to some young lawyer, disintegrating the community of the neighborhood. The cost of rent and soup from the deli would go up and I, like others, would no longer be able to afford it. Then I'd feel like a loser, incapable of keeping up with the pace of gentrification. Now the woke weekenders would have to watch a cult film like *Frankenstein Junior* or *Mean Girls* on some rooftop with peeling paint in Brixton or Peckham for twenty pounds, popcorn not included, surrounded by people exactly the same as them, while the local residents would be forced to go elsewhere, to make space, to avoid conflict.

I was one of them, and I wasn't. The only difference between me and them was that I knew Liz.

On that first day she appeared at the door as everything I had ever wanted to be: slim, sinuous, thick red hair, snow white skin. She glided barefoot around the flat with the ease of someone who was born rich; she wore a red robe with embroidered white flowers and bat sleeves, which swished on the floor as she walked, a glass of wine in one hand and a joint in the other. There wasn't a hair out of place and her face was peppered with freckles. She hugged me like a sister and invited me to leave my shoes outside the door. I asked her where she got her amazing robe from, and she answered that the silk was organic.

Liz had inherited the flat from her grandmother, an English lady who was very respectable apart from when she drank, who had been considerate enough to die at seventy so that her beloved granddaughter would never have to worry about paying rent. She had also left her plenty of money. Liz cheerfully told me these things while showing me the various rooms. I struggled to follow the flow of her words and in my faltering English I asked, and your parents? But she didn't hear me.

She had skillfully paired the inherited furniture, which was a bit dated, with modern minimalist pieces: vases, lamps, and rugs in earthy, muted colors, soft shapes and an excessive number of plants. She was very good at handling beauty. It came naturally to her because she perceived it as part of herself. That was the first thing that attracted me.

The room she was renting out was small and dark, with mold stains in the corners, full of delicious but pointless objects: shapeless ceramics, a glass bottle with dried lavender in, a mandala from Urban Outfitters on the wall, a dark green rug in the shape of a crocodile next to the bed. I lingered for a moment on these details. I knew that I would do anything to live there: I was already hopelessly enraptured by Liz, by her movements, her dreamy yet careful way of speaking, aware of the effect her aura had on her surroundings. I didn't yet know the difference between what a person is and what others see, and my conviction that Liz was simply perfect hung around for a long time. She, on the contrary, didn't seem struck by me; I must have seemed so provincial. I didn't know what to do to impress her and I was afraid that my desire for approval was seeping out of my skin in desperation-infused sweat.

A few minutes later we were sitting in the garden: a damp but wonderfully decadent square of grass. Liz had prepared a short questionnaire to decide whether or not I was the right person to share her flat with, and thus to some extent her time and life. Like in all big cities, proximity was a fundamental component of any relationship. On Tinder you looked for love within a radius of a couple of kilometers—that was the radius of intimacy. The Italian barman at the Queen's Head, the pub at the end of the road, was occasionally my lover, sometimes my therapist, often my father. I don't think he knew my name but he'd say *Are you alright, love*?, and I'd feel special.

What kind of person are you? Liz asked, looking down at the sheet of paper. Until that point I hadn't responded well to her questions: I hadn't seen the TV series she talked about, I didn't read much and I didn't listen to podcasts. I hadn't travelled. All of those things horrified her.

I don't know yet, I responded. A vulnerability that I would soon learn to hide, but that she seemed to like. She looked at me with renewed interest.

Your surname doesn't sound Italian, she commented.

My father is Moroccan.

Oh, cool! She exclaimed with an energy that might have concealed a thread of resentment, as if she didn't expect that from someone like me. I want to have mixed-race children, she declared, I've already decided. I want to fall in love with a North African chef who lives in Paris, so we can take the train to see each other at the weekends, each of us maintaining our own lives, because I can't just uproot myself for a man. It would be perfect, because then our children would grow up trilingual, with Arabic and French, and everyone knows that mixed-race people are naturally more attractive than normal people, like Zendaya or Lenny Kravitz. Have you read any Zadie Smith? You speak Arabic *and* French, I imagine. We should totally organize a trip to Morocco. I've been there tons of times, one of my friends has a villa in Marrakech, but it would be amazing to visit with someone who knows all the authentic places. These days everywhere has been swallowed up by tourism, places get ruined to make everything more instagrammable for us white people. It's weird if you think about it. You go often, I guess. Is your family still over there? I have Scottish and German heritage and the first time I went to Berlin I felt such an intense sense of belonging that I thought I'd been born again. Do you know what I mean?

I didn't say no, I didn't know what she meant because I'd never set foot in Morocco and I didn't speak Arabic or French, because you had never had time to teach me, because you were always working and life was already hard.

I'm an ally, she revealed, and I didn't understand. I intuited though that to be her friend you didn't need to talk much, and that was a comfort to me. She put a glass of wine in my hand. She wanted to know everything about me, she said, and thankfully she interrupted me immediately.

She was kind, generous, beautiful, rich, and powerful, and I couldn't believe she had chosen me.

I still wonder what convinced her, in that first meeting, that we would become best friends. I knew a lot of rich blonde girls in the small town I came from, and none of them had seen me as a project worth spending their time on. But Liz did. She wanted to work on me like on a broken mirror: put me back together, sand down my edges, polish me so that I could better reflect her image back to her. I also wanted this. She wanted to be seen with me in the bars in Soho where interesting people met other interesting people, and I wanted to be seen with her, in the places where it was important to be seen. She wanted to advise me on what to watch, what to eat, and to tell me what was right and what wasn't. She was always available to explain things, to illustrate aspects of the world that I didn't know. She talked to me about feminism and about how it's connected to the class struggle, and lent me books to read that didn't make me feel stupid like I did at school. I was happy to learn. She took me along to exhibitions of new Afro-descendent artists and to concerts where sad women sang heart-wrenching songs and all the girls swayed to the rhythm of sisterhood. She always paid and I always followed gratefully. She encouraged me to educate myself and she scolded me if I made observations that weren't sensitive toward this or that minority until I stopped doing it. She introduced me to her friends, she pulled me out of the shame of my obvious loneliness. She gave me dresses she no longer used, and when we ate out she always bought the wine so that, she'd say, we could get a nice bottle. I spent a lot of time staying silent so that I'd appear more intelligent than I was, but in the silence I seemed to change. Liz reminded me continuously that I had to aspire to be the best version of myself, while I dreamed of becoming her, and I liked thinking about how I would feel then: safe and happy.

Thinking about it now, I realize that Liz lived suspended in an eternal adolescence of privilege and false rebellion. Her egotism was the natural individualism of city life: it was necessary for survival, which meant it couldn't be considered a defect. Everything about her seemed to say *I am*, without ever having to apologize, ask permission, or question herself. I had never imagined you could live like that and now, watching as she smiled at herself in the mirror, I wanted it too. I wonder now what she was like when no one was looking, but it's a silly question, because each of us only exists when we are seen, and she made sure she was never not seen.

Sometimes I peed in her conditioner bottle and shook it up. It wasn't mean, I told myself, because her hair never seemed to suffer as a consequence, but for some reason I got a strange sense of wellbeing from it. I was trying clumsily to rebalance the invisible weights that held me beneath her. I did other things too, like filling up her carton of soy milk with normal milk, which she was allergic to. I saw her running into the bathroom a little while later with her hands clutched over her stomach. But it wasn't mean, I told myself, because she recovered quickly. One time, I went shopping with her and as she passed me things from the changing room—they all looked great, she'd buy the lot—I told her I'd wait at the till and ran to swap them for a smaller size. I asked myself why I was doing it—I felt sorry, I felt guilty, I thought: she's your friend, you can't hate her. But I did hate her. I hated her because I envied her all those things she thought she deserved just because she had them: her skin, her house, her security. At the same time, it was crucial that she loved me, because it was her I wanted to be like; it was her I wanted to impress. I had never had a friend before and her attention quickly became something I couldn't live without.

Sometimes I would get into her bed and we'd fall asleep, holding one another. In those moments she was like a child: she whispered in a high-pitched voice that she was scared of the dark and she was happy I was there with her. She made me feel part of a secret game, just the two of us. We sought refuge in one another, safe from solitude but also from the risk of real intimacy, which we carefully avoided. Our conversations were always interesting and never dangerous. We never talked about our parents or our sad teenage years. I was unaware of her insecurities, and she ignored mine. We were alone together, in the shelter of our shadows.

Sometimes we touched each other. Her body fascinated me; I wondered why it was so different from mine. Hers was more beautiful. I don't know why she did it—perhaps she too wanted to be part of something. Perhaps she too, deep down, was looking for a refuge.

3.

When I went back into the bar, Liz had ordered us another glass of wine each. I thought about leaving, but I couldn't feel my legs. There was something strange in my breathing. I thought I had killed you myself, perhaps, because I wasn't sufficiently sad. I looked at my hands to make sure where was no blood.

What's up? Liz asked me. Are you O.K.? Honey, you're pale.

I shrugged my shoulders. I didn't want to tell her; I knew it would make her uncomfortable. We had been friends for almost six years. I liked it when she talked about herself, but when she looked at me, I felt observed and invisible at the same time.

I told her it was my mother, that someone in our family was unwell, that was all. A series of banal phrases followed, pronounced with false naturalness.

It's my father, I added. I don't know why.

There was a pause, then Liz looked me in the eye, resting her chin on her hand, observing me like you would observe an abstract canvas in an art gallery or a cute puppy picture.

We've never talked about your family, she observed, her voice delicate, controlled.

I was taught that it was rude to talk about yourself, I mumbled, staring at the bottom of my glass. It was red. Was I drinking your blood?

The phone rang again. I rejected the call.

Who's Aisha?

My sister.

What! I didn't know you had a sister! She exclaimed, offended. How had I never mentioned my sister?

Really? Meh, we don't talk much. We had an argument when I left Italy.

Why?

I shrugged. Because I was leaving, I said.

Liz liked it when reality worked in alignment with her understanding of the world. Envy, you see?

Yeah.

She didn't like feelings that weren't nice. She loved the idea that she could choose what to feel and when, at what level of intensity, and for how long. Sometimes, she'd say, she gave herself a maximum amount of time to be sad or angry when something horrible happened (she was never in a bad mood without good reason). Once that time was up, she would simply stop being sad.

Bitch.

What?

Nothing, sorry. In that moment I thought, maybe I'll strangle her. Kill her. I could hit her with the bottle or the glass or the fork.

You're behaving weirdly, she probed. She didn't like being kept in the dark. Meanwhile, my sister was looking at you laid out dead on a stretcher; maybe she was discussing the possibility of an autopsy with the doctor, giving Berta her drops, calling me. I didn't know anything. I didn't know that this wasn't the first time, or that you had a problem with your heart, or that the cardiologist had told you to go on a diet, to stop smoking. You hadn't told anyone. You were all eating dinner together and Aisha noticed you were pale. You laughed in that way you did, open-mouthed, like a bark that comes straight from the depths of your throat, and said: it's nothing, don't worry, I'll go to the bathroom and wash my face, maybe it's the heat. Nobody noticed it, not until afterwards: you planted your hands on the table to push yourself up, and maybe you moved the chair abruptly, dragging it noisily across the floor. Maybe you hesitated for a thousandth of a second at the door, wanting to say something. Worse: if I was there, if I'd been there, I would've understood. These aren't things you think, not even in a whisper. They're things you think when your father turns to ashes.

She was already thinking about your last wishes, the various aspects of the funeral, the types and prices of the tributes, the death notice, the clothes. She was calling me.

Sorry, it might be better if I go, I said, getting up. My hands were shaking. I added that I had to call my sister back, to find out how you were, but I don't know if I said it out loud or not because I couldn't see her: in front of my eyes was me as a child, the evening I refused to eat the soup and you gave me a slap and told me that you were dying of hunger at my age, and immediately afterward your body in a pool of blood, and then the blood on my arms. I closed my mouth and felt a surge of vomit coming into my throat which I held down, then swallowed, the acid burning.

She didn't offer to come home with me and I was glad of it. She had a date with a man of Greek heritage who on his Tinder profile stated a passion for the theater and the gym, and for his photos had chosen one of himself in Rome, one of himself at Machu Picchu, one of himself with his cat, one of himself without a shirt but in an ironic way. Anyway, he had sculpted, hairless pecs, so worth putting on display.

See you at the flat, she said, hugging me.

I nodded with my mouth clamped shut, scared she would smell death on my lips. Once home, I should have booked an Uber to take me to the airport bus, then boarded a flight, transferred at Rome, took another flight. Aisha would certainly have come to pick me up, because she's the kind of sister who always thinks of everything despite having much more on her plate than other people.

Once I was out of the bar, I no longer knew how to not think of you, so I made a list of all the times I had disappointed you and convinced myself that you hated me. I tried to rebut myself, saying you were my father and probably loved me, but these considerations only made my ruminations spiral. I felt my heart beating in my stomach while I thought of every time you had told me off, every time that, sitting beside one another, we had been incapable of speaking. What day of the week was it, how old was I, did I still have a fringe? Memories have to be accurate, if they're not accurate they might as well have happened to someone else. I needed to remember everything, otherwise nothing had happened at all.

I bent over to vomit in a recess. A couple walked past without looking.

4.

The sea air slapped me across the face; I could already feel my lips drying. Sirocco, I thought. The laundry needs covering.

Aisha was waiting for me in the car. I jumped in like a kid coming out of school, hurrying to close the door so the driver behind wouldn't get angry. Southern Italians behind the wheel are always angry. I sunk back into the soft seat, wanting to be enveloped by the upholstery and disappear. Wanting a car to hit us there and then, our car's metal body to crumple and turn us to mush and for everything to end like that. I sighed. Our eyes met in the rear-view mirror: Aisha's face was long and tired. Mine was round and stained with red.

I've booked you an appointment with the beautician, was the first thing she said.

I've already done it, I replied.

Even your arms?

No, but I ran them over the hob. They still smell of roast chicken, here. I put my arm under her nose and she grimaced.

I was an early bloomer: my body hair grew long and black, so thick that when I waxed my armpits, already at thirteen, my skin broke out in tiny droplets of blood. Back home, women's things were done in a certain way, and it was the same for everyone. Female bodies had to be invisible, tamed, appropriate—identical. From your hair to the way you dressed, there was a very specific code to follow, and transgressing it was a risk. People noticed anything that was out of place. They noticed me and my body that never quite fit.

When I left home I stopped shaving, and it had come, in some way, to define me as a person. Liz found it disgusting but, as a good feminist, she was careful not to say anything. But I wasn't doing it for ideological reasons; it was more the remnants of a repressed adolescent crisis, a delayed desire to transgress.

I don't understand why you don't get lasered, said Aisha. A lock of copper hair escaped from her hijab and, in a moment of distracted innocence, she pursed her lips and blew it out of her eyes.

Because I'm a feminist.

Of course you are.

There was a moment of silence as we both evaluated whether to launch into an argument, but Aisha decided to let it go. Sirocco, she said, changing the subject.

Have you covered the laundry?

She glanced at me, amused, and I felt a shiver of familiarity, a quick intimacy I was no longer used to. I looked down.

Do you keep the laundry indoors getting moldy over there?

We have a tumble drier.

I settled into the seat, got my sunglasses out of my bag, put them on, turned towards her, pinched her arm, then envisaged how, if we swerved just then, we would fall straight into the sea.

So you have a machine to replace sunlight and you think that makes you better than me?

No, I'm better because I'm free.

Aisha gave me a look that made me feel, as always, deficient. Freedom doesn't exist, she said. The only thing that exists is choosing your cage.

And are you happy with yours?

Mina, it's only a fucking scarf. You're an Islamophobe. You should be ashamed. Papà has literally just died.

Papà didn't give a shit about that stuff.

You have no idea what Papà gave a shit about.

And you did?

At least I was here.

Right, let's get this out of the way then.

Free. Can't you see the price you've paid?

I stared out the window at the piles of trash people had dumped on the side of the road. Clapped out buildings, concrete columns still visible. Illegally built houses. One-story buildings, peeling walls. Faded paint. The smell of sea salt, gas hobs, sauces simmering on a low heat, dirt, sweat, ashes. The smell of death. A strange buzzing, like the sound of time passing. Everywhere, the sea.

Hey, I said, why don't we stop for a minute at the usual place.

Aisha sighed: I promised Berta we'd come straight home. You know how she is when she's left alone with Nonna.

Come on, I just want to stretch my legs.

She took the usual exit, pulling into an unpaved road, and parked in front of a wall that had a hole in it, around a meter and a half in diameter, a sort of tunnel that you had to crouch down to enter. It was scary when we were little, because among all the bits of trash lying in there were mice and infected needles. Now we went through without even looking. We'd both seen worse.

On the other side of the tunnel was the sea. It was dark like the bottom of a well at night, gashed with white by violent gusts of wind. It was a nasty sea, unpredictable and capricious, playful and childish. Hundreds of people drowned in it every year. Behind it, the volcano. The sun that fell upon the sea, the earth. Raucous, stately seagulls. A lone fisherman on a rock. Children in the distance playing, holding a noose made of grass to catch lizards.

We sat on our usual rock. When we were younger and the sea hadn't worn away so much of the beach, the boulder rose up dry and warm a few meters back from the water; now we had to get our feet wet to climb onto it. In that same spot six years earlier, I told her I was leaving and she slapped me and refused to cry. Losing a sister is like losing half of yourself. I couldn't explain to her, then, that I didn't want to betray her, but I had this need, this tick tick tick in my head that told me: you have to be new. I called it freedom.

She took a tobacco pouch from her bag and pulled out a joint. She lit it and passed it to me, staring at the sea that forgives all.

I asked her about the plans for the funeral.

He wanted to be cremated and scattered at sea, like a non-believer. As if all the in-between had never occurred. She took the joint from my hand, took a drag, and exhaled into the wind, her eyes moist. My insides were tied in knots.

Nonna thinks she's back in Emilia during the war, she said suddenly, and I saw a hint of a smile I used to know, of when she found something funny, but knew she shouldn't. I thought of the way you laughed when someone tripped and fell and broke their teeth. I can't even remember the last time I heard you laugh. I wasn't there for things that were funny when they shouldn't have been.

Oh yeah? What does she do?

Well you know that her carer lives with us now, right? She's convinced she's Jewish. I know, I know. She's Polish, and they're all Jews to her. Don't give me that look—basically, Nonna thinks Magda's Jewish and every time she hears a loud noise she starts shouting at her to hide in the wardrobe because the Nazis are coming. She says she can see them coming round the corner from the window. You have no idea how many times I've had to pull poor Magda out from under the bed.

She didn't tell me, though, about the times Nonna had shit herself or when she got lost one afternoon and they thought she'd gone forever. Some things I didn't have a right to know; I had given up the intimacy of the everyday, the ugly bits. Old age is about presence. I would've struggled with taking Nonna to the toilet, I thought: isn't it sad to feel repelled by my own flesh and blood, by a decay that foreshadows my own? A mirror to my own.

How's Berta?

Aisha exhaled heavily through her nose like a cat. Her face was tense. She had had to restrain herself our whole lives, because there were already too many emotions in our house: tears and screams and too loud laughter. She didn't like loud noises; she often hid herself away in dark corners. We'd find her curled up under the bed or sitting in the wardrobe. When we were little, we slept together and I wanted to hug her as if she were my doll. I suffocated her. I suffocated her with hugs and kisses, and with my nightmares. I would tell her all of it, but I never asked what she dreamed of.

Berta spent hours on the phone with her spiritual guru, Aisha said, then with her analyst, then with the woman who reads her tarot, then with the doctor because her psoas is hurting. At the end of all the phone calls, she's tired, has a headache, stuffs herself full of pills and sleeps for fifteen hours. I don't know if she's really realized what's happening.

I think I know how she feels. I don't think I've really realized what's happening either.

Aisha burst out laughing. What are you doing here then?

I missed the sea.

You could've gone to Brighton, she retorted.

I didn't respond. I got down from the boulder and crouched a few centimeters from the breaking wave, my hands ready to catch it. I saw the smooth stones under the water, clear and bright even though it was almost evening. I heard the sound of pebbles pushed backward and forward in my body like a call. I withdrew, spooked by the intrusion.

Let's go, I said, and walked past Aisha without looking at her. I didn't want her to recognize me.

5.

The house was still the same. Surrounded by a low, dirty-white wall, covered in graffiti of generic insults—they had never bothered anyone, apart from me, who took everything too seriously. Aisha opened the gate. In the garden, the tangerine tree had gotten older but was still thriving. Berta told us you'd planted it when she got pregnant with me—it was my twin tree, a bit acidic, a bit lopsided, but full of fruit and hardy over winter. The rusty swing chair had a new flowery cover. Bottle green window frames. Salmon pink walls, tarnished by time, by the wind, by neglect—who would re-paint them now? At the door the smell of wood and incense, the worn-out doormat, the cats waiting for me. You were no longer there; you were everywhere.

I immediately felt an unmistakable familiarity with the space around me: a total understanding of the way things and people were in this place, as if nothing here could surprise me, and at the same time a feeling of total unfamiliarity, a painful separation from the me who grew up in this place, because the person I had become was irrelevant here.

I don't trust my memories; they are always infected by the present. They're shy. I chase them, chase them, chase them, never knowing if I remember a thing for how it was, for how it made me feel, or for how it suits me to tell it in this precise moment.

Nobody has ever confirmed that my memories correspond

to how things really were. When Aisha and I talk about something that happened, we often find ourselves telling it in very different ways. We don't have photos, Berta wasn't there, you are dead. Nobody in the city saw. My memory is pure fantasy. I don't know whether I had a happy childhood or an unhappy one, or if there were alternating moments of happiness and unhappiness, like in everyone's.

We lived in a house by the sea, in a provincial mafia-run town that had once been called one of the best villages in Italy, but not much had changed since then. I remember the sound of the waves and the gulls in the mornings, and my sister's hot body next to mine; the sounds of her sleep. I remember Berta getting into bed between us to wake us up; she was small and fragile and too young and perhaps she wanted to be our sister too and that someone else would look after all three of us. I remember rays of sunlight streaming through the curtains and how we would try to catch bits of the dust that bobbed in the air with our fingers. Berta would blow raspberries on my stomach and I would wriggle around laughing, the whole bed shaking. Eventually we would drag ourselves down to breakfast, with the window open and the sounds of the sea floating in. When the wind was hot, we'd close the window to prevent the house from filling with sand from the desert or the volcano. You had already gone out. You always got up very early.

Before school I would come and say good morning at the bar, which was on the way. You were always happy behind the counter, with your friends, your secret languages. Your friends worked at the market and their faces were always tired. I found them a bit scary because they were dirty, but they were always very sweet to me. They taught me how to drink mint tea the way Berbers do, sipping loudly, as loudly as I could. You would tell me stories that I believed only because you'd told them. Your eyes shone and you would put a hand to your forehead, as if to keep all your memories safe inside. You'd bring me behind the counter, into your world. You had two hats, a witch one and a wizard one, that you hid in the kitchen and every so often we'd put them on and pretend to make potions with spices. You'd sign my late notes.

You'd put a hand behind my neck and pinch my skin, distractedly. I felt like I was yours.

Then, when I grew up, my body changed. It didn't look like Berta's body or Aisha's or yours; it had curves and lumps. I hid it under big black dresses that made me look like a garbage bag. I stopped coming into the bar. You didn't understand and I'm sure you were hurt; when you tried to hug me I'd wriggle away because I didn't want you to feel the bulk of my erroneous body. You would timidly tell me I was beautiful, and I never believed it. I no longer wanted to invent concoctions behind the counter.

When you saw me walking past the glass door of the bar, I'd see you start and raise your hand, but I'd quickly look away and walk on. I was becoming a person who was detached from you, with my own imaginary world, which wasn't the same as yours and which I was ashamed to share with you because it was suffering and solitary, a knot of inadequacy and fear. Our relationship started to change, to lose itself, to become entrenched behind the Do you remember whens, too embarrassed to ask Who are you now?

When we went inside, Berta was upside down, her heels against the wall, and she stayed there. If she wasn't my mother, I might have found this woman interesting and eccentric. But she was my mother, and so I found her selfish, unreliable, and fickle.

She wasn't only this: a woman is not only a mother. Nobody is only one thing.

She had been, before anything else, a disappointing daughter: to my grandmother who was as cold and severe as a soldier.

Berta was a delicate child, with a sickly disposition, watery eyes and pale, irritable skin. She was allergic to the sun; she had to put on liters of lotion just to go out into the garden. She seemed to always be in the wrong place: she should have been born in the north of the country, into a quiet, intellectual, kind family, who would have sent her to dance classes. Young Berta would perhaps have liked a mother who tied up her hair in colorful bows and played the piano, who spoke softly and wore shoes with a heel so she could be heard before entering a room.

But she was born in a partisan house and brought up later in the suburbs, austere and at the same time noisy, unfriendly, a house of survivors, of violent communications, and closed doors. I don't know exactly what her childhood was like. I only know that when my grandmother speaks to her, Berta shudders almost imperceptibly. Berta is always tired and doesn't like leaving the house. I know that she met you by chance and that she thinks you saved her life. I know that she had me at twenty-four, and that I at twenty-four would certainly not have been a good mother. Nonna hadn't been one to her; nobody taught us how to love.

Nonna was thirty during the Years of Lead. She had seen the war as a child and played it as an adult, because that was all she knew. She lived in Rome at the time and hung around in smoky circles that she never talked about. She slept with many other grimy young people like her and believed in violence. Berta was born in that period, and perhaps that's why Nonna never loved her. She continuously left her with neighbors and acquaintances as if she weren't hers, and when she had to go back into her arms Berta would cry and cry as if she were a stranger, because children always know when they're not safe.

Berta had grown up not knowing what her mother was fighting for: a war that seemed invisible, a war of ghosts against ghosts, of ideals, fought with low-grade weapons and hunger. She didn't like it, and when she had the freedom to have an opinion on whatever she wanted, she didn't, to protect herself. She didn't read *L'Unità* and she wasn't interested in politics. She cared about frivolous things, out of spite for her mother, because all daughters dream of being nothing but the opposite of the woman who created them. Nonna left her alone so many times that Berta didn't know what it meant to look after someone. She had never known her father and, when she asked after him, Nonna made an angry face and told her she certainly didn't need a father, or any man, because men are weak and stupid and have an unloaded pistol between their legs.

After the case of Aldo Moro something changed and Nonna, who only ever thought about survival, packed her bags, pulled Berta out of bed in the dead of night and, without saying goodbye to anyone, returned to her hometown, to an old house by the sea that had belonged to her father's father. There they commenced a different life that consisted of breathing the same air but never talking. Berta watched *Gone with the Wind* and *Doctor Zhivago* and cried. She was afraid of everything but the sea.

When I entered the house, I didn't think of any of these things, because I wanted to hate Berta with all of myself and feel no compassion for her. Since I was young, I had been used to speaking primarily to her feet, given that she was often standing on her head to make her bad thoughts slide out onto the floor. Her feet never responded and sometimes smelled, because she always walked barefoot and never cleaned the floor.

Berta, I said, rigid. I hadn't seen her for a couple of years, perhaps. I hadn't called her mom for at least ten. I didn't remember the last time she'd hugged me.

Aisha, well accustomed to softening the tension, tried immediately to lay down some ground rules: Mom, get up, say hello properly. Mina . . . Try not to act like a guest, okay? This is your house too.

Berta did what she said like a well-trained puppy. She looked at me and for a moment I thought I glimpsed a jolt of resentment, of horror. She felt something toward me, I knew it, but she wouldn't say it.

Have you cried yet? She asked instead, and then took a couple of steps back to get a better look at me.

You've gotten chubbier, she added.

Berta reached a hand out toward one of my braids, but I recoiled as if her fingers were white-hot. I thought: what if I hurt her, like really hurt her. I come from her. I thought: if she doesn't love me, who ever will? I thought: I'll die alone, they'll find me days later, when I start to reek. I thought: Berta will die. Do I want her to die? Do I want her to die now? She only cared about you, though, didn't she? She has always only cared about you. Do you want to take her with you?

I felt a stabbing pain in my stomach and my vision fogged over for a few seconds. My throat was dry. I felt my fingers, toes, and ears become numb.

Have you cried yet? She asked, again. There was something in that question that perhaps I didn't understand.

No. But I've been throwing up and shitting liquid for the last two days.

She nodded like it was the most obvious thing in the world.

It has to come out somewhere. Drink some water and cumin, then smell an onion, she instructed in a practical voice. If it wasn't Berta I might have thought it was the voice of a mother.

Witches' potions won't sort this out, I mumbled. I was afraid to look at her; I was afraid to see her come undone before my eyes.

There's nothing to sort out, she said. Life is unfair.

She got back into position and resumed her practice, breathing noisily. I hated her. I hated her for her selfishness and insensitivity, and I hated her because hearing her regular breathing throughout the house comforted me like a balm.

6.

I told work I had to take some time off for family reasons. Nobody asked any questions.

I was the director's assistant at the Angel headquarters of a fast-food chain that's very popular in the UK—Bagels—famous for their avocado toast and the enthusiasm with which the cashiers greet you when you walk in. The city's 9-5 workers considered it a healthy and affordable option: a chicken and avocado toasted sandwich cost £5.45, and if you added a piece of fruit or a dessert, and maybe a ginger-flavored drink, it would come to about £10.

I had started out in the kitchen, cleaning and prepping sandwiches. On my first day I was given a handbook that contained everything I needed to know, from which and how much detergent to use to clean the surfaces to detailed images of how to assemble the salads. On the wall there was a timer that went off every five minutes to remind us to wash our hands and disinfect all the worktops. Bagels is an extremely clean, perfect place. If the yolk of an egg wasn't an intense enough yellow, the whole thing was thrown out. Salad, if slightly brown, was discarded. I often had the impression that I too, like those limp lettuce leaves, would sooner or later be ditched.

After a few months I graduated to the front of house: cashier, then barista, and finally assistant manager. I had experienced every promotion as a recognition not of my work, but of my worth as a person.

At the beginning I hardly spoke English, but I knew how to smile on demand, and I learned the necessary lines by heart. There was a script to follow, and precise movements. The customer had to feel loved as if by a caring, ideal mother who never scolded, never neglected, never made mistakes. My only desire in the world was to give the middle-aged man who had his hand down the front of his pants—dozing immobile on his dick—his soy cappuccino. The lecherous way he said *darlin'*, or the way his hands rubbed against mine as he passed me the money didn't matter: I was in love with the customer, with every customer, and also with life, and with this city, and, above all else, with Bagels.

It's essential work, human work, inclusive work, my manager told me. You can be the difference between a good day and a bad day for someone. He also informed us that every potential customer could be a mystery shopper sent by the company, evaluating our store's performance and giving us a score. A high score meant that at the end of the month we would all receive a gift card or even a cash prize. A low score meant the whole team would get a demerit. It was a big responsibility, because I knew that Conchita in the kitchen was a single mother with five children, and that Eddie always needed cash—he needed to buy coke to do in the toilets to get him through the 5 A.M. shift.

There was competition between the various Bagels in the city, because every month the best one was in with a chance of receiving a significant prize. We won once and, adding a bit of our own money, we bought tickets to see Florence and the Machine. It was the first time I'd won anything in my life and I was ecstatic. It was also the first time I went out with my colleagues and for some reason I thought that something would happen: that I'd be recognized for who I really was by a group of my peers, and that would enable me, finally, to recognize myself.

But that's not how it went. We talked about the usual things. We were very different people: a mixed group in terms of age, origins, and education, and the effort to find things we had in common tired us out pretty quickly. That new Netflix series, the Peruvian restaurant in Shoreditch that was the new place to be, work gossip. We ended up complaining about our boss for an hour, then went into the venue, grateful that the time had passed and that we wouldn't have to talk during the show.

It was my first concert, if I didn't count the local festivals back home. I was very excited before it started, trying to imagine the effect it would have on me. But when Florence walked onto the stage a strange thing happened: I felt so many emotions at once—disappointment, joy, nostalgia, sadness—and despite the fact that I was surrounded by so many people, I didn't know who to share these contradictions with, contradictions I suspected nobody would understand. I didn't want to catch a colleague's eye; I also didn't want to let them intuit what I was experiencing. I didn't have anyone's hand to squeeze, I didn't know what to do with my body, how to interact with the mass of strangers all around me. I saw other people shouting, clapping their hands, moving their heads and shoulders, even hugging and kissing. Existing in that moment. I thought my heart might stop, there, all of a sudden, and that I'd collapse dead on the floor, and it occurred to me with terrifying lucidity that nobody would know who to call. On the bus home I burst into tears in a noisy and vulgar way, wheezing. Snot fell onto my lips and I wiped it off with the sleeve of my jacket—nobody would notice, and nobody would offer me a tissue anyway.

I thought about phoning you, in that moment. Maybe you had felt this way too. But it was late and I didn't want to wake you. I didn't want to highlight that this was the life I had chosen for myself. That maybe I'd made a mistake, that I was afraid I was living badly; that everyone around me seemed to manage, but I was failing. You had managed to make a life with much less. Would you have told me that people who choose to hurt themselves aren't allowed to cry?

I avoided thinking about it. This was my life and it needed to go on.

With the city I maintained a relationship of subservience, like unrequited love. I loved her, but I didn't know why. Sometimes I ran in the park alone, went to the top of a hill and looked at the skyline that lay beneath. I heard the beating of my heart in my ears. After work I went to an English class, and with time and Liz's help I became good at it. It was thrilling to be good at something. When the course finished, I signed up for other evening classes. Gardening, ceramics, random things. More than anything else I liked the idea of redeeming myself for an education I had always refused. I would go to the free taster lesson then drop out. I didn't want to learn—I wanted to observe and study other people and life.

There were times when the streets were silent. One night I crossed paths with a fox: she stared at me and I stared at her. She, like me, was an alien hidden in plain sight. I had always felt alone, and now I was alone among many. I crossed the city without worrying about how I was dressed or what color my skin was. I believed nobody could hurt me. I absorbed the external until I could no longer define my edges, and the more I felt myself disappear into the weave and weft of the streets, the bare brick, the parks, the intermittent chatter that floated out for a few seconds from an open then closed door of a pub, the safer I felt.

My days melted into one, like a house of mirrors in which I didn't know how to—I didn't want to—distinguish between myself and my reflections. I bought my ticket for the merry-go-round. I told myself I could go on losing and reinventing myself forever, without ever truly trying to find myself. Weightless, sticking to nothing, fluctuating through time and things, things that mattered and things that didn't.

Aisha phoned me sometimes to ask how things were going and what I was up to. I responded that everything was fine and I wasn't doing much, because that was the truth.

7.

The town was small, but all the things I would discover later, in the city, could be intuited there with surprising clarity: the importance of the shape things were meant to have, for example. A family had to have a square shape in which no corner was hidden from the others. From outside it had to appear strong and unassailable like a castle surrounded by a moat. That's how we were. It was important to protect yourselves from the other, from their wickedness and "malanove," as the Calabrians say.

Appearing was important, and it was also important not to appear. Neither too happy nor too sad. Proper, composed, modest, not drawing attention to yourself. Arrogance attracts envy, and envy brings misfortune. Misfortune brought on by arrogance is a misfortune that's invited—deserved, predestined. You had to follow certain rules to not draw that kind of gaze: the evil eye. Clothing was important. Jeans paired with sweaters in simple colors were O.K., or a branded tracksuit—Nike or Adidas, or a plain dress with a soft black or beige coat over the top. Other things were important too: your hair, your eyebrows, your body hair, your fingernails, your scent. Everything had to be carefully attended, but not *too* carefully. Your body had to be thin, but not too thin. Your way of speaking was important, like avoiding dialect if you were from a good family. And then there were the common-sense rules of decorum: eating with your mouth closed, not chewing gum in public, covering your mouth when you laughed or, better still, avoiding laughing too much, just smiling, not making too much noise. To the question "how are you?" you never answered "good," but rather "not bad," or even better, "I can't complain." Don't complain, but don't be happy either. Everyone in the town was fearful of the judging and malevolent eye of everyone else.

Berta was not up to respecting these rules, so she hid herself away. She didn't go out shopping; she didn't come to parents' evening, or to pick us up from school. If someone caught a glimpse of her in the garden or at the beach, she would hear whispers coming from afar and want to disappear, so she didn't eat. I was ashamed of her: she was never neat and tidy. I was the little girl, but so was she. Aisha knew it too, so as soon as she was old enough she tried to remedy all our mother's shortcomings: she learned to cook and clean and darn and she would ride me to school on her bicycle. I would sit on her baggage rack with my legs to one side and wrap my arms around her waist.

Berta came to pick me up from school once. I was with the girl I sat next to, who I thought was my best friend. In reality she was indifferent and barely tolerated me. Sometimes I went to her house to do homework after school. Her mother treated me with excessive generosity, imbued with a sense of superiority that I wasn't capable of understanding at the time. She often asked if I was eating and gave my friend an extra sandwich for me every day. My friend swapped it for a sugary snack which she wasn't allowed at home. That's why she tolerated me, because the compassion I inspired in her mother was useful to her.

I was with her that day when I saw Berta. She had those stupid braids and sunken eyes, her thin face unmade apart from electric blue eye shadow and lipstick that was too red and jumped out of her pale skin. She looked like a clown. Maybe she'd put this make-up on especially to come here, to the school gate. I wished so hard that she wasn't my mother. I didn't want the others to see her: I knew how cruel children could be with their words, and indeed they were.

* * *

She was not a simple woman, my mother, not just because of how she dressed, or how she laughed and moved and smelled, but mostly because she was born outside of marriage and her mother didn't dress her like a girl when she was young. Then she married a Moroccan man and went mad. Or maybe she was mad before she married him. In the town, people whispered various versions of her story; I didn't know which one was true.

In the town simple women were the only acceptable women. "Simple" was the biggest compliment: it meant wife, it meant mother, it meant servant, it meant silent, it meant unimportant, it meant invisible. Becoming a simple woman demanded a lot of work, which varied depending on your social class. A woman of modest extraction was simple by definition, as long as she was careful not to be vulgar. Vulgar were those who flaunted their poverty with malice or their wealth with scorn.

For a girl from a good family, on the other hand, to become a simple woman meant first and foremost to be studious but without ambition, which was uncouth. She could be intelligent, but only if the intelligence embarrassed her. It was preferable to work very hard but not stand out. Girls who finished high school and were from a good family went to university, financially looked-after, in Rome or Milan. After graduating, they would prepare for the teaching exam. They would become good teachers who smoked secretly on the fire escape between lessons.

Work was obviously important, but a career wasn't, because the career of a simple woman from a good family was marriage, where the only potential promotion was motherhood. The parents of girls from good families would help the newlyweds to buy a house. The mother of the girl from a good family would say: we have made so many sacrifices, but the children are happy, so we can't complain. She would visit often to help out. The daughter from a good family would become pregnant within the first year of marriage. She had spent her whole life studying and maybe she would wonder why. Or maybe she wouldn't. That's how girls from good families became simple women. After a few years the couple would set about returning to her hometown, to raise the children near to their grandparents. She would request a transfer to another school and he would take over from his father-in-law who could now retire to leave him a thriving business—a law or accountancy firm, a dental clinic, or a GP surgery. Worst case scenario: a tobacco shop.

The mothers took the children to school, the same one they had gone to; to the same little parks they'd been molested in at fourteen by some old man who lived nearby, but they never thought about it and sometimes convinced themselves it hadn't really happened, that it was just a dream.

Fashions came and went. The girls from good families followed them, resupplying in the same shop where they had a tab and paid in installments. They had layers in their hair, which was just a little bit wavy and not too long. They talked with the other moms about vacuum cleaners and recipes for Christmas dinner, and complained about how tired they were.

Doesn't your husband help you? One would ask, malice flashing across her face. Why of course he helps me: he hangs the laundry on the furthest line that I can't reach, he sets the table when dinner's ready, he sometimes loads the dishwasher as he has his method—he's much better at it than I am! They would laugh happily, watching their children play. At birthday parties they'd compliment the host mother's organization, saying: You always overdo it! How many dishes have you made?

If you paid for outside catering you were lazy; if you made the cake yourself you were a cheapskate.

That's how simple women grew up and lived in the town, while Aisha and I were never invited to the parties or the parks or to any other place. We were wild girls, but it wasn't something to be proud of. Perhaps this is what Liz sensed and envied in me, she who worked so hard to imitate the freedom that comes from neglect.

Nonna wanted us to study, but she did nothing to help make it happen. She shouted when I came home at the end of the school year having failed, needing to retake Latin and math in September. She had a quick-tempered and nasty character which would every so often pour out of her, uncontrolled. I gave her constant opportunities to express her rage and I felt this gave me a right to secretly harbor my own. When, at school, I had to respond to a question or take a test, I would feel it boiling up inside me and would always end up failing. I don't know if the failure was predetermined by our socio-economic background, or if I simply desired it for reasons I couldn't explain.

Everyone blamed Berta—mothers are always to blame—but she had no idea. She got up in the mornings after I had left the house, and she was often still in bed when we came home, in the darkness of her room. Even if her eyes were open we had to take off our shoes so we wouldn't disturb her.

Would you have preferred a girl from a good family? But you chose her, and she was so grateful to you for it, maybe too grateful. Did you love her? I like to think I was born, if not from love, at least from hope.

8.

Being home made my face itch in the mornings. I felt like I was suffocating, and thought constantly of the city: its red bricks, its tree-lined roads that were pink in the spring, the composed hurrying of its people, their indifference. Going into shops and not being able to afford to buy anything, but observing the beauty of the objects, the idea of possessing.

I constantly stalked Liz's profile on Instagram. It was important for me to keep updated on what she was doing. I had only been away a few days but already felt a strange tension germinating between us. I didn't tell her you had died, even though she was always asking for news. She updated me on all the wonderful things she was doing and I invented just as many for myself, because suddenly I didn't want to be less. I felt that the distance engendered a competition that when we were together would have seemed ridiculous. But now I was in Italy, and as far as she knew I was practicing yoga and meditation every morning with my hippie mom, volunteering at the migrant center, playing chess with the old men on the beach at sunset, and all the other things that could be distilled down to the hashtag #slowlife. I knew her routine from memory, and it was perfect, like she was.

She got up at five in the morning, went for a run, then, walking home, called her childhood friend, who she went to dance class with when she was little. It's important to maintain friendships, she'd say, especially female ones. Once she was home she'd have a shower, with some podcast on in the background where women talked about being women in a world made for men—but with a candor that was reassuring and prevented them from coming across as angry or unpleasant. These women complained about all the things that happened to other women—never to them—and on which they always had something sharp, ironic, and brilliant to say. There was one podcast in particular that was in one of Liz's lists of recommendations, where successful people talked about their failures, which were always infinitesimal within the context of their successes. I didn't know if I was the only one who saw the contradiction, or if I was just a loser.

At that point in Liz's typical day, it was seven o'clock and she could devote herself to reading while sipping her coffee. I often photographed her then, with the rays of sun streaming through the window, her transparent body curled up in an armchair as if it were a crib. She pretended not to notice. I would post the photo to my profile and feel proud that I had a friend like her.

One time, we had a conversation that has remained impressed on my brain, because of the almost-terror she reacted with: I asked her at breakfast whether she'd like a slice of bread with Nutella since I was making one for myself. She replied, with a look of shock on her face: I always eat muesli with organic almond milk in the mornings.

And what if one morning you felt like something different? A croissant, say?

I always want muesli after my run; it gives me energy and makes me feel clean.

O.K., but . . . what if one morning you didn't feel like going for a run? What if one morning you didn't feel like doing anything?

She smiled in a controlled way, tense like the string of a kite in the hands of an anxious child, then went on: I could never live like you do!

I asked her how I lived, and she said I lived badly. You don't really care about anything, she said. You eat unhealthily, don't work out, don't educate yourself . . .

I shrugged. There are things I care about, I mumbled.

Yeah? Like what?

I care about—I responded with an uncharacteristically rebellious ferocity—eating what I want when I want.

I didn't know it yet, but I wanted her to envy my radical freedom, my softness, my difference. I had something she didn't: a bedrock to sit on while she tirelessly ascended towards the ideal body, the ideal career, the ideal life, the ideal ideal.

Liz would then cycle to work, arriving a few minutes early, just in time to go to the bathroom, get undressed, wash her armpits, look at herself naked in the mirror of a sterile, alien space in which she would never wonder where the scissors were, where the razors were. Who knows what she thought when she looked at herself. She'd put on her Urban Outfitters bra, one of those ridiculously uncomfortable lace ones with no hooks, wiring or padding, designed to make you feel you are free. Then a geometric patterned top, open just low enough to be able to see the lace underneath, so that everyone knew she wore a feminist bra and not the kind that caged her in. She'd put her sports top in her *New Yorker* tote bag—she had a subscription but only read the cartoons—and put that into her Fjällräven rucksack in the summer, or her Rains one in the winter. She'd greet everyone with a smile. Liz always smiled, like someone who knows they are well-liked. Life, in her head, was like being in one of those giant pools full of white plastic balls.

Far from the city and from Liz, I no longer felt I had an identity to lean on in order to exist. I looked around me and what I saw no longer contained me. In the metaphor of a vase shattering on the floor, I was not the vase, but the water. If I stayed in my hometown for too long, I would risk discovering that I was different from the me I had constructed in the city. I found the prospect terrifying; everything reminded me of something else. The sea irritated me with its familiar odors, and its dramas of childhood. I couldn't stand the slow hours, I didn't want to sit with Berta with my eyes closed, I didn't want to read Morante with my grandmother, I didn't want to recognize the practicality and the wisdom of Aisha's abrupt gestures, and I couldn't stand my desire to help her, my desire to participate in the reconstruction of a world, our world, in which you were no longer, but in which, despite myself, I belonged. The mirror in the bathroom, chipped in the left-hand corner, where I still saw myself as a child, reflected a nasty gaze. Did I look at everyone like that, or just myself? And the sink into which the water flowed, smelling of salt, water that dried out my skin and hair, and Berta with her rings that clinked in the kitchen the rare times she washed the dishes, whispering to herself shanti, shanti, shanti. The plates had to be washed before seven, because in summer that's when the water stopped. When we came back late from the beach, we slept with our salt-wrinkled skin. We stretched out, encrusted with sand, on the living room rug and played rummy. You taught us.

In the evenings I watched Berta attentively, because I was scared she would die and I wouldn't remember the last time I'd seen her. She sat on the bed in her flowery night shirt. She was so short that her feet dangled above the floor, only her big toe brushing the parquet. She whispered mantras to herself: things that served no purpose. She'd sit for a while, then curl up under the covers and fall straight asleep, the light still on, barely breathing. She was surrounded by photos of you, but she didn't look at them.

I pushed away the instinctive familiarity with which my body moved inside that prison space. The mint in the garden, the cats that settled on my naked stomach when I napped in the afternoons, the muggy heat of late June, the sunsets over the sea, bumping into my elementary school teacher in the supermarket, her greeting me with affection, without hesitation, because she had recognized me from afar. You've always had the stride of someone who knows where she's going!, she said. If only it were true. Solitude is a form of absence, and in my case it was I who was absent: I felt this emptiness in the core of my body, and I was grasping, grasping, to fill it up. I began to remember who I was before I left and discovered, painfully, that there was nothing special about my pain: I was cracked as a teenager, and a teenage crack never fully heals.

There were still things we had to do that kindled in me the secret, surprising pleasure of taking care. Secret because to reveal that pleasure would be too much of an exposure. In the kitchen, a colony of rice moths fluttered around in and outside the cupboard, unaware of our grief. Behind our backs they ate the food we deprived ourselves of, like a silent and poetic natural chain that replaced us for that period when we didn't know how to live our lives. Aisha and I decided to get rid of them one day, because we wanted to cook rice pudding, the way you used to on a Sunday evening when we were little. Your mother, you told us, would make a kind of soup with milk and semolina, black pepper and oil, but it wasn't easy to find the right semolina here, and rice absorbed more, became creamier. It was our favorite dish in the world, and you were very proud of it. Sometimes, with small, simple things, you brought us into your world.

We set to work clearing out the kitchen. It was a meticulous act of liberation—a purge—but it was also the exhumation of a body, the skeleton of something that had once been a family.

We worked in silence. Every so often I looked at Aisha furtively, hoping she would burst into tears or break a glass, or start screaming like a madwoman. I wanted her to show outwardly what I felt inwardly, what I was working so hard to keep caged in, not wanting to bother anyone. But if she'd given in first, I could have done it too without being told I was too emotional. But Aisha gave no sign of feeling anything. Her face was focused and, her hair gathered in a messy bun, gloves up to her elbows, she seemed so normal, so ordinary. So beautiful.

Sometimes my mind returned to when we were little, in our bed, and we talked about the things we could do to look like rebels. We painted our nails black and pretended to smoke chewing gum cigarettes. Then I carried on being a rebel, alone, and she gave it up. I betrayed her and she betrayed me, or we simply grew up too far apart to recognize one another.

Maybe we were thinking the same thing, because after a long silence I heard her chuckle her sad laugh.

Do you remember when we cut each other's bangs with nail scissors?

Of course I do. The teacher nearly fainted.

And you took the blame; you said it was your idea but it wasn't true, it was me who wanted to do it.

I shrugged. They didn't care how I behaved; I was already a weirdo.

Aisha's eyes softened and I looked away, fearful of seeing pity in them, a compassion I absolutely could not accept. I was suddenly inundated by painful images. My school report lost among the chaos. I had been held back in math, and only Nonna had shouted. I would have blown myself up to attract the attention of you and Berta, but you looked at me as if you were looking at Saturday night TV, your minds elsewhere. Sometimes Berta didn't get out of bed for days, and you told us she was sick, and I was scared she was going to die, and at night would go and check she was still breathing, putting a finger beneath her nose and feeling relieved when the air tickled my skin. When I left, my duffle bag on the doorstep, Aisha refused to leave her room. I needed to catch the bus. A goodbye at the door, silence from the other side. I was twenty, she was twenty-three. She was already working with Papà. She had finished high school with the highest grades but couldn't afford to carry on studying, because Papà needed help. It was she who should have gone away—she was smarter than me, braver, she hadn't wasted years searching in the reflections of windows.

But Aisha was too loyal; she would never have left you. I, on the other hand, the wretched daughter, abandoned you, and now, to punish me, you have died without warning.

After a few seconds I risked looking at her again—she was reaching under a shelf searching for something, a circus of rattling pots and pans.

What are you doing?

I hid a pack of cigarettes under here somewhere.

You're almost thirty and you're still hiding things?

You're almost thirty and you're still using sarcasm when you feel vulnerable?

Meh, there's nothing to drink in this house.

Aisha found the packet, passed me a cigarette, lit one, and exhaled the smoke slowly while leaning against the kitchen wall. This is where we learned to walk. This is where we told Berta about the school plays she wouldn't come to, the grades she wouldn't remember; this is where Mamma had a headache, over there is where she went to lie down.

This character you enjoy playing, she said, slowly. Isn't it tiring?

I felt winded. It isn't a character, I said. We can't all be good little nuns like you. There are people who can live without some omnipotent god telling them what to eat, what to wear, and what to be grateful for.

Aisha looked at me in a way that made my stomach turn.

I don't understand you, she said, and for an imperceptible moment her voice trembled. You go on and on about living in the most cosmopolitan city in Europe, right? About how you spend your time with all kinds of people, how you're in intimate contact with all these diverse realities, all peacefully integrated, or whatever. Your Instagram looks like an awareness campaign. And yet you can't bear my faith? What has Allah ever done to you?

The idea that women have to cover themselves so they don't tempt men is just a form of oppression, you can't deny it.

She shook her head. It's just a symbol. Why do you dress the way you do? Don't you also have something you want others to see? I'm sorry to disappoint you, but this is who I am. I don't feel oppressed.

Come on, Aisha, you can't claim that Islam is progressive when it comes to women . . .

But it isn't about religion! Some governments use Islam to maintain power and promote their bigoted ideas, but the religion is just a means. If we followed the Gospel to the letter, this country would also be a hellhole. The patriarchy is a system and it will use anything it can get its hands on to sustain itself. I am not less free because I wear a headscarf; I am less free because I wasn't encouraged to study, because I have to hide my ambitions under a layer of moral modesty. I am less free because nobody asks my opinion on political events, only what I've cooked for lunch and where I bought my boots and when I'm going to find myself a nice boyfriend. Because tampons cost a fortune, because there isn't enough research on endometriosis, because airbags are designed for male bodies, and when we were young they taught us that Einstein was a genius and that we have to be thin to be desirable. Do you really think you're free? Please, I was there when . . .

Yes, I remember, thank you.

We had to go to a different region.

I said I remember.

A silence full of resentment fell between us. Aisha wiped her upper lip with her finger. She always sweated there when she was angry.

Sorry, I shouldn't have brought that story up. It's just that sometimes I don't know who you are. I'm sure you would never say something this superficial and nasty in the city. I bet you're always respectful to people of different faiths and minorities there, when it suits you. I don't know who brought you up.

Nobody. Nobody brought me up.

And that makes you feel authorized to . . . to . . .

To what?

Aisha shook her head. To judge.

I can assure you that I judge myself much more harshly than I judge anyone else.

She rolled her eyes, watching the smoke floating upward. That doesn't make me feel any better. How you see yourself is a reflection of how you see others. For some reason you feel a need to make me feel inadequate, and there's nothing to justify it. I don't care if you feel you're a victim. We are all victims of somebody. But I don't need this, not from you, not now. If you have a problem with my scarf, keep it to yourself.

Sorry, I mumbled, ashamed. I did have a problem with her scarf. I had a problem with her having stayed. I had a problem with the thought—persistent, snarling like a hungry beast—that you loved her more than you loved me, because she fell into line and I fled. She was a martyr, I a deserter. She was devoted, I a traitor. I fled and I lost myself, I lost everything.

You want the truth? I sighed and turned toward her. From the way she looked at me I knew she saw me. I felt violated by her gaze. The truth is that it's good that you have the veil, because it means I can think that you're less feminist than me and less free than me, and less modern and less independent and less I don't know what else. Because otherwise I'd feel like an amoeba, a slobbery snail without a shell, a slimy thing that everyone is repulsed by and nobody loves.

I felt my hands trembling and I squashed them between my thighs like I did in high school to hide my panic attacks. Aisha noticed but pretended not to, and I was grateful for her tact.

I don't know if God exists, but I like talking to him. He always forgives, always understands. It's like talking to the gentlest part of me. Nobody taught us how to love ourselves—this is the only way I know.

She wasn't explaining herself. She was talking to me, maybe for the first time, about herself. Then she continued: how is it, really, to leave?

I thought about it, then I said, hesitantly: When I was here I knew exactly who I was, because I saw the differences between myself and other people and I didn't feel understood. I didn't accept myself, I didn't love myself, I couldn't see myself, but I knew who I was. Then I went there and it was like . . . starting again as a completely different person, a version that was truer than the truth. I felt lost but I had chosen it, and I liked my suffering, because I was alive and I was alone and I could decide to let myself go and nobody would stop me. There were moments, sometimes, when I'd sit in a park or a pub and hear the buzz of the people and close my eyes and feel truly free. I don't know who I am anymore. Every day is different. Nobody recognizes me, nobody looks at me. Nobody cares about my body hair, that I've left the house in my pajamas, whether my hair is tidy. Which means these things no longer exist. Sometimes I look at beauty outside and I feel beautiful too, but only in its reflection. It's all outside of me, and I limit myself to admiring the image I've created of my life, but I never know if it's real or not. I look at it and say: it's such a beautiful picture, and if I'm living it, it must be true, right? I must be at least a small part of it. Sometimes I say something in English and people laugh because they understand me, and I feel like I've grown ten centimeters taller.

How is it to stay? I asked her. I never wondered that, the

idea of finding out scared me. The only formulation I let myself consider was that if I had stayed I would have died of boredom, trapped in a place that would never have understood me. But I didn't want to think about the luxury of time, the ways I would have spent it. Who with.

She shrugged. Staying is like time passing, and you watch it pass and perhaps you change or perhaps you don't. She put the cigarette out and stood up, taking my hand. Come on, let's go to the bar, I'll show you.

9.

The bar was called Tangerinn. It was a few blocks from home and opened out onto the beach. From what I recall, it has always been noisy, crowded, and full of smells that were always new. It was frequented by all the immigrants in the area—and only as I got older did I grasp that if a place is frequented by immigrants it is not frequented by anyone else. I wonder if this ever bothered you, but you certainly didn't make a big deal out of it. It allowed you to recreate the atmosphere of the home that you'd lost, you tried to reproduce its smells. In the mornings you served msemmen with cheese and honey, at lunchtime koftas, tagine with chicken, lemon and olives, and on Fridays you made cous-cous. You were cooking all day and all night, handing down secrets. Mint thrived in our garden, meaning you could always have a pot of tea on the go.

At the beginning, the bar was my favorite place, purely because the people there didn't look like Berta, like my teachers, or like my classmates. They looked more like us, like you and me who had inherited your skin. But as I grew up, I understood that you and I and those like us were wrong. Your friends seemed dirty, and I felt dirty too. So I washed obsessively. I didn't understand why Aisha and Berta were lighter and you and I were darker, but I knew that, whatever the reason, it was bad. Your friends wore old, threadbare clothes and smelled of the market, of fish. But they were always laughing and when I came to the bar they embraced me like I was the daughter of all of them. I was scared that their smell was also mine. They taught me to play chess and rummy. They loved me and I loved them too. But they were different, and I didn't want to be different. I didn't want to be like them, like you. I wanted to be normal.

In the eyes of the people from the town, immigrants were all the same. But being different from the whites didn't mean they were all the same. The people who came to the bar had lived a huge variety of lives, spoke languages that were nothing like one another, sometimes as distant as Italian from Finnish—yet they were all bundled into the same box. The members of a minority don't have the luxury of being themselves: in the face of power, they become only difference. To contain multitudes is a privilege, to be incoherent is a privilege, to be unique and unrepeatable is a privilege. To be and to belong at the same time is a privilege.

When Aisha and I were little, you were an "extracomunitario." That's what people from outside the EU were called then. At that time "extracomunitari" immigrants were mostly Albanian or Moroccan, by which I mean that anyone who came from the former Yugoslavia was Albanian and anyone from North Africa was Moroccan. The women who came from Eastern Europe looked after everybody's grandparents, because they were white but cost little. The Arab women struggled to find work because the rich people in town didn't want them in their houses: they said they wasted too much time praying and refused to do the dishes or clean their bar carts. At best they found work cleaning the stairwells of apartment buildings. The Moroccans sold tissues at traffic lights or, if they were lucky, had a stall on the market. Some were passing through—heading north—but most stayed because they recognized, in the ambiguities of the sea, a place in which they could live, suffer, and die in peace. Interactions between immigrants and locals happened only at the market, and nowhere else. People who lived by the sea were welcoming, but only to those who feared their own God: they were suspicious of all the others. The fact that their God was the same God as the God of those other people they didn't even want to hear.

After all, they had their own problems, what with the trash in the streets and the illegal building sites and the pizzo to pay and the shops randomly blowing up. The people who got shot at random, for being in the wrong place at the wrong time. And then the trials, always unjust, they said, always making an example of someone, even if he had nothing to do with it: acquaintances, neighbors, good people, small fish. Businessmen can't do anything without ending up inside, people would say. A mere signature could fuck you over. Then everything would return to usual. Every so often a film or TV show would come out. Middle-class people would talk about it indignantly: we're not bad people, they're always bad-mouthing us, this is why tourism isn't coming down here, there's beauty here too. The pride of the community seemed to be awakened only when it was criticized, never to defend itself from itself.

It sometimes happened that some immigrants ended up embroiled in these things, because easy money is appealing to anyone. Then a Moroccan disappeared, and nobody asked questions.

We didn't know what was going on—fish don't know they're in water. You were no different. You believed in survival at all costs. I never asked you about the compromises you had made, because I didn't want to sully my conscience with the truth.

And you never talked about it. You never talked about anything.

10.

As soon as I set foot in the bar I was ensnared by your smell and felt my knees give way. I saw you fall to the floor hundreds of times a day, and now I had your smell too to add to the realist scene that was obsessively playing out in my head: you falling, you calling me, me not hearing, far away, paralyzed, an inert observer unable to reach you, you already a ghost.

Behind the bar there was a boy I didn't know. He was black as tar and had sweet, shining eyes. I greeted him in Italian. He looked at me shyly and turned to Aisha, who explained in English that I was her sister.

Aisha's English was fluent, natural. She had always been good at languages. The boy smiled at her; he trusted her. He had every reason not to ever trust anyone again, but he trusted her. Aisha volunteered at the migrant reception center and whenever she could she offered work to people she met there. You and she were trying to create a community around that little nerve center of passing souls, misunderstood cultures, mother and stepmother tongues. You with your French, Arabic, and German, Aisha with her English and Arabic learned crumb by crumb—you managed to make yourselves understood, to create space, to embrace. Many had arrived in recent years, more and more afraid, their eyes extinguished, old at twenty. They were men and women who had thrown themselves off the edge, as if their lives were worthless, to save themselves from the monster. Humiliation, pain and, despite everything, hope—always hope. All the way to the sea; the sea that joins life and death.

* * *

He had arrived in Italy a few weeks before, on a boat that set out from Tunisia. He was called Mahdi and he was welcoming me into my own home. I was the stranger.

Your father was always talking about you, Mahdi said, timidly.

That's not true, I retorted. What could you have ever said about me? What did you know about me?

No, really. He said he was proud of you for going away and making a life for yourself, like he did, like we have done.

Not really like you've done, I thought.

How did you get here? I asked, feeling awkward. I moved my weight from one foot to the other and didn't know where to look. I felt as if I were under attack.

He smiled, sadly: I walked. It took over a year.

My eyes opened wide. I thought he was joking, but Aisha warned me with her eyes. Yet he was saying to me, without irony, that he and I were the same; that we had both left our homes to make new lives for ourselves.

There are journeys and there are journeys, I mumbled, and forced myself to hold his gaze, to look at myself in his sad, sweet, black eyes, because something inside me knew that this shame was fair and should be felt.

One summer we decided to spend a weekend in a commune on the Isle of Wight. It was a commune of European "refugees"—frighteningly rich people who, having reached a superior comprehension of what makes man unhappy, had decided to abandon the capitalist lifestyle. They refused to call themselves "expats," as they would have been called in the city; they were first-class immigrants.

They are a group of radical thinkers who want to revolutionize the way we think about consumption, Liz explained in her mellifluous voice. They are running away from the things everybody else is running after. They are people who have given up everything: penthouses and cars and insane holidays, not to mention their clothes. There's a documentary about them on YouTube—I'll send it to you—you have to watch it before we go otherwise you won't understand a thing.

At the commune they grew their own vegetables, which, in the United Kingdom, referred to the sole category of tubers; they foraged for mushrooms, berries, and the few fruits that are able to grow in that politely hostile climate. They lived in close contact with the poop of chickens, an animal considered sacred for its ability to produce eggs. The cows were sacred too, and we had to thank them whenever we drank their milk.

Rich people have this habit of acting like they own every place they go. The "refugees" claimed they had established a relationship of total respect with nature, but they conceived of it as something accommodating and domesticated that was there, simply, to be used. The direct consequence of this idea was that the bucolic lifestyle wasn't enough to sustain them. They were accustomed to enjoying avocado on toast, and despite having ambitions to use their own feces to produce energy and do all the other things you see on TV survival shows, they were too lazy or stupid to make it work. So, to make up for what they couldn't obtain from nature, they had created an area of the commune for "the curious": to give other rich, privileged, and unhappy people the opportunity to ponder radical change. They had erected some magnificent yurts, they had woven blankets, bought matrasses and other boho-chic furnishings from Maisons du Monde, and that was the beginning of the commune's hostel. One yurt for six people cost three months of my salary, but it included all the activities that we were invited to participate in: goat yoga at dawn, a meditation walk with forest herb study, fruit picking, vegan cooking classes, an hour of silence, cleaning the toilet to humble the spirit. Our money, Liz told us, would be used in part to make improvements to the commune itself, and would in part go to a fund for the construction of a school in Africa.

The Wight weekend had obviously been her idea. Liz had selected other interesting women for the experience: almost-friends who she surrounded herself with so that she would never feel lonely. She had brought a bag of MDMA with her so that we could deepen our connection to one another.

We all met at King's Cross station. I spotted her selections a mile off—they were all the same: long, white, and slim, like fettuccine. You'd be forgiven for thinking they were there for a photo shoot. They managed to look both absent-minded and hyper-aware of every pair of eyes that fell on them. Patagonia or North Face backpacks on their shoulders, a symbol of adventurous spirits. I had a worn-out duffle bag, the one I left home with, the same one you left your home with. You gave it to me when I decided to leave, almost like a passing of the baton. Nobody else in the family had ever used it.

I was more attached to that duffle bag than to anything else, but in that moment I felt foolish for having brought it, and for not having spent money I didn't have to buy myself a backpack like all the others. They were wearing winter Birkenstocks on their feet, the furry ones, with Scottish wool socks—the ones they posted on Instagram, in the morning light with a mug, a book, and the hashtag #wintering. They were wearing light dresses or skin-tight lycra cycling shorts, with huge sweaters in earthy colors thrown over, their hair in inconsistent braids. From the waist down they weren't cold. They were heavenly and ridiculous. I was terrified by the idea of having to pretend to be proud of my body, which I hated. I reached for the hem of my dress, praying that what was beneath it would disappear.

The weekend felt like those hot dog eating contests they do in America, but in reverse. Everyone wanted to show everyone else how indifferent they were to material goods and comforts like having a hot shower or peeing in an enclosed space. Deprivation was a point of pride. The romanticization of the simple life—which to me seemed awfully complicated—had to be documented from every angle and shared abundantly on Instagram. Everyone pulled their Hunter boots and Napapijri windbreakers out of their bags and nobody ever got hungry.

On our arrival they explained how we should use our phones: we could take photos and videos, but any posts on social media had to wait until we were home, so that we wouldn't spend the weekend monitoring our like count. They gave us little bits of twine to hang our phones on and a disposable camera that we could use to express our creativity. The others were as eager as schoolgirls at the zoo.

We went to visit the communal kitchen. Men and women who were determined to live in accordance with nature—we were told by Kubra, a young Nigerian chef who had moved there after ten years working in the city—collaborated equally in the sustenance of the commune. She seemed to truly believe in the project, and I felt a pang of sympathy for her. She had a cloud of electric black hair and luminous eyes. She responded to all of Liz's questions with great patience. Liz wanted to know how they got all the essential nutrients into their diet, and in what quantities. Where did they get their protein from? How many carbohydrates?

Liz has always been thin. It mattered to her more than anything else, but she pretended it didn't. She always talked about how she didn't do anything specific to maintain her thinness. She said she had a quick metabolism and she used ideology to camouflage all the tricks she employed to guarantee herself a slim body. Liz didn't eat meat, didn't eat dairy products, weighed her portions out using scales. She wanted her food to be "clean"—she said it helped her to concentrate—and she worked out to make herself feel stronger. For the entire duration of mealtimes, she nibbled sparingly at a piece of bread she held in her hand.

We aren't so precise, Kubra shrugged, but you should talk to our yoga teacher, Esme. She used to be a nutritionist, and she's the one who deals with any problems of malnutrition. Her next class is in half an hour, so you might find her in the gym.

The gym was a smelly tent in which Esme was laying out the mats and smoking a joint. Liz asked her if she could interview her for her channel and she agreed.

You see, diet culture was killing me, she began without hesitation, as if she had given the same speech a million times. I was meeting so many mothers who were bringing their teenage daughters to me to teach them how to eat and the idea was always the same: they had to aspire to a slender, underweight body. Nobody cared about their muscle mass or the layer of fat that protects you from injury or the ageing of skin. I think I have many eating disorders on my conscience, not least my own which, as you can see, is not fully under control. At that point she lifted up her t-shirt. There was something truly strange in that gesture. She seemed aware of the problem and at the same time wanted to exhibit it. She liked her body, because it was thin, but at the same time she was ashamed of it, because it wasn't free.

Liz stared at her ribs. You have no idea how much I get you, she said, and she confessed that she suffered from orthorexia nervosa. It's when eating healthily becomes an obsession, she explained. I eat too many vegetables, work out too much, have too healthy a lifestyle. Don't get me wrong, it makes me feel good, I feel amazing. But sometimes I envy people who just eat what they want, like Mina. She doesn't care at all.

Esme looked at me and I shrugged. Don't superimpose your experience onto mine—she said to Liz, serene but firm—we have absolutely nothing in common. She walked away without adding more, without even giving Liz an opportunity to respond.

Liz fell silent, unsettled. I wanted to laugh, but I said nothing, and after a few seconds she recovered. She put her arm around me and whispered: this woman needs help, she doesn't seem like a balanced person. Did you see the way she lifted up her shirt? It was gross. Who would want to see something like that?

Later on, Liz said she didn't want to go to dinner. She was lying on the bed with two cucumber slices over her eyes; an intense scent of lavender arising from her half-naked body.

I took a photo of her with the disposable camera and she smiled at me, satisfied. I asked if they could bring us some food so we could eat here instead, she said. She pointed at a basket full of cheeses, eggs, and various nibbles. I wondered whether whoever had assembled it was thinking of their TripAdvisor reviews.

Liz pulled her MDMA out and took a dose. Then she passed the bag to Ashley, who imitated her without hesitating. I was scared of drugs, and since nobody was watching me, I hid my share in my pocket.

Half an hour later the girls were naked and dancing to a sad song by Blood Orange. I sat on the bed; I hadn't gotten undressed, and I tried to appear at ease.

Mina, you're so silent! Tara said suddenly, sitting on the floor next to the bed and looking up at me with curious eyes. You haven't even told us what you do.

What you do—what you do in life. In any conversation, in any context, it was *the* question, the only one that mattered, the only one whose answer people remembered. Tara, for example, had a degree in history of art and worked on humanitarian projects for a tech company. She had just got back from Nepal, where she had supervised the construction of a singing school for orphans. In the photos she showed us, she was surrounded by happy children wearing t-shirts with the company's logo printed across their chests.

I work for Bagels. I'm the manager's assistant, I replied, and I coughed because I realized my voice was weak and betrayed all my feelings of inadequacy.

Oh, cool, Tara responded, and looked away.

Isn't it super refreshing how Mina just isn't ambitious?, said Liz. They had all moved closer and were looking at me with curious eyes.

To explain truthfully what I thought about ambition, I would have had to speak about the me from before, and I never spoke about the me from before. I would have had to tell them about you, about Berta, about Aisha, about what school had been for me: a cruel place where I never felt safe, in which every look could be followed by a word, a scornful laugh, a judgment, violence. I was afraid of how people looked at me. A teacher once told me I was like the engine of a Ferrari trapped inside a Fiat Panda. Wasted potential. Maybe she intended to spur me on to work harder, but at the time I interpreted that affirmation as an immutable fact, sealing my nauseating suspicion that I was an alien: my shell was wrong, and my engine was going to break down. When I moved to the city and met Liz, I thought it was finally ready to be scrapped.

I said nothing of that, obviously—instead I cited an article from the *Atlantic* that Liz had sent me a few weeks earlier and of which I had read only the infographic on Instagram. I said that ambition is a privilege; that the West attracts migrants with promises of self-realization, selling them a narrative of success at all costs in exchange for labor. Meritocracy doesn't exist. Liz looked at me with the satisfaction of a mother at a school play. I received that look with a gratitude that was probably excessive. Berta had never come to my plays.

Emma, who came from Poland and had received a Soviet education that constantly poured out of her mouth, despite currently wearing the equivalent of two salaries in clothes, nodded enthusiastically. She was a fashion photographer. She had pastel pink hair, cut very short, and dressed like a woman from a magazine with thick-framed, rectangular glasses, crop tops even in the winter, and eighties tweed jackets that were two or three sizes too big. Underneath, she wore pants that looked, to all effects, like her father's pajamas. Regardless, the effect was extraordinarily sensual.

Liz smiled. It was thanks to her that these exchanges were happening, thanks to her that our useless chatter deceived us into thinking we were contributing to some theoretical change. All that surrounded her was nothing but a mirror.

With all due respect, I disagree, said Ashley, who I already knew because she had vomited various times on the lavender in our garden after mixing alcohol with lines of cocaine. She worked in the sales department of a luxury brand.

It was a conversation they'd already had many times, but everyone loved repeating it because it made them feel intelligent. Everyone, myself included, dutifully played their part.

I think the magic of living in the city is that whoever has a dream can cultivate it, realize it, and be rewarded for their efforts, Ashley continued. I obviously agree that the difference in starting points is unfair: until everybody has the same opportunities, we can't talk about *real* meritocracy. But you can catch up in the race, and the city allows for that. Take you, for example: you arrived here barely speaking the language and with all probability you'll be a manager within a year.

I believe we should all aspire to improve ourselves, because the wellbeing of each of us flows into the wellbeing of all of us, said Liz, placatory.

By improving ourselves, do you mean improving our

economic conditions? I asked in a quiet voice. She wasn't expecting it. She stared at me for a second with her mouth open.

It's human nature to change and evolve, she replied. If that instinct isn't there you get stuck and unhappy. Unhappy people love blaming others for their unhappiness, but people who are satisfied with their lives are satisfied because they know they have worked for that life, that they've won it for themselves . . .

. . . that they deserve it? I concluded, with a smirk. Liz shut up.

But you do realize that ambition is a trait that gets inculcated into children depending on their social class? Emma intervened, filled with fervor. Ashley squeezed her hand with condescending affection. They had been together for two years at that point; Ashley had bought a house for them both, an enormous house with a room that Emma had transformed into her darkroom. It's not an innate instinct: it's something you learn. Lower class families don't teach their children that they can have everything in life, because they know it's not true. It's easy for rich parents to send their children to private schools, enroll them in the best universities, and pay for them to realize all their dreams, and we call that merit? It's pure and simple privilege!

Well of course, Emma, Ashley cut her off. You don't need to state the obvious. We're all in agreement here.

There was a moment of silence in which Ashley was surely pondering the fact that Emma could only afford to be a bohemian artist because she earned two hundred thousand pounds a year. We were all thinking it, not least Emma, who after a few minutes returned to defend her point of view, on which we were all in agreement, without even brushing on the contradiction between her ideals and her lifestyle. Ashley and Liz smiled and Emma, embarrassed, turned to me: What do you think, Mina?

Liz responded like lightning in my place: Mina isn't the political type, are you? It's not an ideological matter for her; she's just lazy. In the best way, obviously. She's just not interested in success.

I felt myself turning red and I wanted them to stop looking at me. I looked down and nodded. Liz decided that argument time was over and changed the subject. After a few minutes I went outside to smoke a cigarette. I walked through the field listening to the sounds of the evening. Suddenly I glimpsed the unmistakable light of a screen in the dark: it was Kubra playing Candy Crush in the silence, her shoulders leaning against a low wall, next to an enormous black plastic bag. I moved closer and looked inside: it was full of empty packages of expensive ready-meals from Marks & Spencer.

Don't tell anyone, she whispered without looking up from her screen.

I burst out laughing.

Can I ask you something? I asked, and sat down next to her. Why are you here?

She carried on with her game. I felt lonely, she said. Being lonely is the worst thing, don't you think?

I nodded slowly, and asked: Why is being intelligent and ambitious more important than being good, or generous, or kind?

Kubra sighed, pulled her eyes away from her game and looked at me for a moment. I don't know, she said. But if you're referring to your friends, they don't exactly seem like geniuses.

They're not exactly my friends, I specified. Just people I know.

I wish I had been strong enough to take something good for myself away from that episode—perhaps to realize that I was stubbornly following the ways other people lived rather than asking myself what I wanted to do with my own life.

Instead, what I did when I got home after that weekend was spend half my month's wages on a new backpack.

Aisha was watching me anxiously; she wanted my approval but she would have never asked for it. I looked around: the smell of mint and spices filled my eyes with tears. It was all very different from last time. The bar was the same: a long, heavy wooden countertop with the grooves and knots of a still-living tree. But behind it the walls were embellished with Moroccan zellij tiles, and the sink and the kitchen counter were copper. There was a light-colored parquet floor and low tables in various colors. The chairs, all different, looked like they'd been taken straight out of kitchens from the seventies. The atmosphere was relaxed; under the silence there might have been anger but also gratitude. Everything coexisted here. Some of the small square tables had a chessboard painted on top. I could see you playing against yourself—you often did that. Who knew who you were talking to under your breath. Were you lonely? Had we left you alone with your memories? Or was it you who closed yourself in, forcing us to look at you from the outside?

You've done well, I whispered to Aisha, who had already positioned herself behind the bar and sent Mahdi to make some kofta and toasted bread. I sat down at the bar, in the same place I used to sit as a child, in the mornings before going to school.

Aisha smiled at me, her eyes shining as if she had been awarded a Michelin star. I swallowed. I felt both guilty and inadequate: Aisha had stayed, yet she had done something good with her time. I, on the other hand, didn't think of time at all, obsessed as I was with place.

She showed me the menu—it changed with the seasons and all the ingredients were from nearby. She had built connections with local businesses; she even showed me photos of happy cows in the field of the farmer who supplied the milk and beef.

But we also have vegetarian options, she hurried to add. We do language exchange aperitivos in collaboration with the University for Foreigners, and a bunch of amazing initiatives with Doctors without Borders and Save the Children. We're a base for the various communities who arrive from Lampedusa. We also organize beach volleyball tournaments and stuff like that . . .

Her voice trailed off, she waved a hand, as if to say, "it doesn't matter." You're not interested in these things, are you? she asked. She looked so fragile, like a little girl again. She still nibbled nervously at her bottom lip, a throbbing open wound. I leaned over the bar and hugged her.

You've done well, I repeated, you've done well, you've done well, you've done well . . .

She pushed me away, quickly drying her eyes.

I'm sweaty, she said, don't hug me.

When we were little and we took baths together, you'd always do a little poo in the tub and it would float there until Berta noticed it and started shouting like a hysteric.

Yeah, well. We've grown up since then.

I shrugged. She was still the same—stubborn, brilliant, loyal. I hadn't missed her. I had my own life. I looked around and didn't recognize any of it. I told myself that maybe this place was a bubble: Aisha had made it welcoming and colorful, the voices in languages I didn't know made me think of the city. But this wasn't reality, I knew it. I knew how people looked at Aisha in the street. I knew what they said about her, about us, about you. What they called us.

I felt it in the pit of my stomach, when as a teenager I walked with my eyes lowered. Aisha was like a skyscraper next to me, her spine was long and she was proud. I, on the other hand, was scared. I felt that my skin was different in a way I couldn't explain; I was a mixture of things that each had nothing to do with the other. I was mixed, hybrid, polluted. I heard them whispering that my mother was strange, that she had taken an African into her bed, that she was a whore, that she was crazy, that you were using her, that we were unnatural. I heard them, but maybe it was me who was whispering those things. And you used to say that it didn't matter what people said, but I wasn't like you and Aisha. I felt constantly observed, the judgement of others a paranoid ticking in my head.

Aisha looked at me hesitantly.

We have to talk about it; you know that don't you?

About what?

About what to do. With Papà. With all this. She spread her arms out to indicate that she meant the bar.

What do you mean? You keep doing what you were doing, and I go back to where I came from.

Aisha sighed, and suddenly I realized how tired she was. She was carrying the weight of a devastated family, her shoulders were bowed, she had black grooves under her eyes like inken scars.

She took a paper envelope out from under the bar and handed it to me.

Part Two

1.

When you were young you never wondered whether you were wanted. It wasn't a question people asked, you didn't talk about things beyond your primary needs. Life was extraordinarily simple: the little you had was the little you knew. The smell that wafted from the kitchen on a Friday. Playing soccer. Teasing Zahra for crying at every little thing. Since your sister Iman married an Egyptian and moved to America, Zahra was the only female in the house other than jidda. You never thanked her for protecting you from feeling what she felt so sharply: that you were lost or, more accurately, fatherless.

Your father was a ghost even when he was alive. He was a proud and silent man, and his presence in the house felt restricting. You would speak in low voices in front of him and eat with rigid shoulders. You never saw him laugh, you had no secret language, no code that you could've interpreted to give yourself the answers that an eight-year-old needs. The only memory of him you had was the time you bumped into him outside the house, not long before he died. Jidda had asked you to pick up the bread from the shop on the corner and you were proud to obey, like a young soldier sent to his first battle; you must have been six at most. Jidda usually asked your older brothers for help with household chores but this time she had asked you, and you were delighted because jidda was your queen and all you wanted was to serve.

Al-jidd was on his way home from work—you wanted to

ask what he did all day, where he went, whether he had his own office, if the city outside of Derb Sultan was as big as they said, with roads with four lanes—but you weren't brave enough. The neighborhood was everything you knew: a crossing of two perpendicular roads, squat houses with two floors, then an unpaved track, a gas station, a few shacks. You were so far from the sea you had to take two buses to get there. Al-jidd climbed the stairs next to you, in silence, until all of a sudden he put a hand on your neck, squeezed the skin between his thumb and forefinger and called you *puce*, flea, in a low, serene voice, almost as if he were smiling. His grip was firm, but it didn't hurt. With his thumb he drew a circle on your skin, pressing a nerve you didn't know you had but that would torment you for the rest of your life. When he took his hand away it was as if he had taken a piece for himself. From then on, his hand was like a phantom limb. You felt it on your neck; it kept you awake at night.

You had one photo of him. You kept it hidden like a secret treasure. When you left, you left it with Idris, the youngest. He didn't have memories of al-jidd because he died when he was born, which meant Idris was maybe the one who suffered the most. You and the others knew you had a father, even if he was a ghost, whereas Idris felt he had popped up like a mushroom, the son of nobody. He was shy around jidda; he didn't trust her. She spoilt him in an attempt to make him feel secure. It wasn't a good strategy, but it wasn't her fault: she didn't know how angry Idris was, angry and hurt for having been born that way, a leaf without a branch.

He was the only one whose birthday you celebrated. This was the privilege you envied most. You too wanted to be celebrated, but you didn't want to have to ask. When you were old enough to get a part-time job at the shop, you bought yourself a cinema ticket and on the day of your birthday you went alone, without telling anyone. You chose a war film because for the same ticket price the special effects looked more expensive, so you were getting better value for money. You thought about the stupid people who paid their five dirhams to go and see a film where the actors just sit around a table the whole time—like paying to watch people in a bar! You were smarter than them, you thought, and you also bought popcorn, which was completely revolutionary—Western. With the remaining money, you bought one of those yogurt drinks on your way home, the ones you had to shake first, and you drank it in one go, as if someone might take it away otherwise, then you met the others at the bar. Like always, they were happy to see you. Samir challenged you to cards and didn't let you win, but you won anyway. You felt like a king.

Idris has probably never experienced that feeling, not even on his birthday. There has always been something missing.

Al-jidd wasn't the only ghost. Of eight children, only six remained: Iman, the eldest, the most beautiful, who had fled to faraway lands and no one expected to see again; Malik, the man of the house, an employee at the Post Office who saved you all from poverty; Zahra, who wasn't beautiful like Iman and cried all the time; Boubakar, the crazy one, the good guy; you, the talented, the arrogant; and Idris, the angry man. Jidda brought you up alone, six children and two dead whose groaning spirits roamed the house. She managed to scrape together a little something here and there repairing and sewing custom-made clothes: formal silk suits embellished with lace and pearls that neighbors paid for in instalments, which they used and re-used and passed down to cousins and relatives. But that wasn't the only thing she was good at: her real talent, the thing she was better at than anything else, was surviving. Jidda came from the countryside. In the countryside women were equal to men in the family and in work, toiling in the fields; they didn't cover their hair and they were often stronger than their husbands. Jidda couldn't read or write but she could do sums and had a kind of historical memory, a popular wisdom that she taught by example, never giving lessons. She spoke only when she had something to say. Otherwise she worked hard and when she was tired she closed her eyes and smiled—another day had passed, everyone was still alive, and if Allah willed it there would be food on the table and she could surrender to her body. She never judged anyone, because judgement brought the evil eye, and she feared both. She wasn't naïve or superficial; she knew the simple truth of being human, that desire is dangerous, and that you live well by simply doing what needs doing and taking breaks now and then to drink tea.

There were a couple of years, between al-jidd's death and Malik's employment at the Post Office, where the family suffered from hunger. Hunger was a feeling: a hollowed-out sadness in the pit of the stomach. Physical, visceral, and mental. A sensation like dying without dying, it changes you. If it goes on long enough, it can turn you bad.

As children, you and Idris argued a lot. There were six years between you: too big a gap for mutual understanding, but too small to ignore one another. He followed you everywhere, like a shadow—he was looking for a figure to idealize and he had decided that figure would be you. But you, still not sure who you were, couldn't sustain such a responsibility: it felt threatening to see a miniature version of yourself reflected back at you. Idris saw you one way while you wanted to be another: two different versions of Omar, you felt divided, not fully formed. While you focused on defining your identity through childish acts of rebellion, Idris followed your every move and repeated them in a way that was slightly more hesitant, slightly more refined. It drove you mad. You hated him when he stared at you with his wide eyes that said: I see you. You didn't want to be seen, not by him, who knew you too well. You wanted to be anonymous so that you could be anything. You didn't have anything of your own but your thoughts, and Idris wanted those too: he wanted to read your mind, to be you. He made jidda sew his jeans the same as yours and in the mornings he waited for you to get dressed so he could wear the same color shirt. He had started at your school, and he wanted to take the same subjects.

The thought that over the course of a summer your clothes would be too tight and you'd have to pass them down to him made you bristle. He blended into you; he nestled comfortably into your warm and roomy character. You were popular in the neighborhood, respectful to jidda; you were talented, you liked to run and to sing. A troublemaker, but caring. Idris, who wasn't a natural troublemaker, tried to make trouble but would then feel guilty and blurt it all out to jidda, every little detail, hoping his remorse would win her over. He wanted to be more loved than all the others, and you were terrified that he was—especially when jidda told him that he looked like your father. Growing up, you found solace in the idea that maybe she told him that to give him an image of his father that he could look at every day in the mirror. But later, whenever you remembered the photo you left on Idris's bedside table before leaving, you realized painfully that maybe jidda told him that simply because it was true.

Papà, where are you when I think of you? What kind of man were you? A man to love or a man to fear?

2.

I remember the moment I knew I had to leave. I was locked in the bathroom and had barely breathed for hours. I knew where the razor blades and scissors were, and suddenly I needed to vomit. The teacher had told you there was something wrong with me, that you needed to take me to see someone—I'd made a fuss because Gianna, who sat next to me in class, said my elbow had brushed against her pencil case and, to get revenge, she'd drawn on me with a black felt-tip. She said my skin was contaminated and I thought I could feel the ink seeping in and circulating through my veins. I would die the moment it reached my heart. So I scratched the black line away with my nails. There was blood everywhere and the teacher was crying. Berta didn't come to pick me up—she never went anywhere—but the teacher insisted that a parent was needed, so you had to close the bar early, losing money. You said nothing in the car; I was terrified I'd disappointed you, but also worried I hadn't managed to get the poison out in time. Maybe it was already somewhere inside me. I thought, for the first time, that maybe it would be better if I'd never existed, and I began to imagine myself dead. I didn't want to die, though, so I left.

At home, Berta had a migraine and we had to be silent. You barely looked at me. I thought you were scared of me. We were just two strangers who looked the same.

Your self-imposed exile was slow and mostly unconscious. You didn't understand what was happening until it happened, even if your memories were strewn with clues, like after the end of a love affair.

When you were sixteen, you believed the world was yours. Your life was divided between school, the athletics track, and the bar: it was a small world that didn't ask for much, but it was yours and it was beautiful.

You went to the linguistic high school and you studied French and German. You liked using another language: it was like pretending to be someone else. You were no longer Omar, the middle child, the troublemaker, the one who would run home after school. You were Omar the marathon runner of Berlin. Omar, the Moroccan singer in the bistrot of the Marais. Omar the young talent out to conquer Europe, the promised land. To your mind, Europe was all the same: narrow streets, arrogance, single plates, wealth. You'd get there one day, and the food, the silent open windows, the too-clean bars would feel sad—but then you'd learn to twirl spaghetti around your fork, you'd discover a calm and gentle sea where you could swim without fear, and you'd learn that the people were kind and similar to you in all the ways that mattered. But back then, Europe was just a game between you and Samir, a fantasy you didn't overthink.

At school, you trained for the four-hundred meters. You'd been doing athletics for a few years at that point, and you had become quite good, but you had the potential to do better. You had smooth, explosive reactions and a lot of power. But that wasn't what made you good. It was the hunger to be the best at something that none of your brothers could do, and to see that mixture of awe and envy in their eyes. It made you feel taller than everyone else. Jidda never came to see you run, and you didn't realize how much it hurt. You looked up and felt a hole in your stomach. Hunger. When you got home, she would listen to your stories, and comment, with a melancholic smile, that you were becoming a man. She said it with pride because it took talent and dedication to grow up.

If I win the championship, I'm going to buy a bike—you said, standing proud—and I'll take you around in my basket!

She would laugh and run her slim fingers through a mountain of semolina, rubbing it distractedly, a lock of red hair falling out from under her hijab. You looked at her like children look at display cases in museums: grubby hands stuck to the glass, eyes wide open. She was the most beautiful, most good, most pure thing, and she was also yours.

You had a special relationship. Your brothers were too rigid, or too grown-up, or too angry; they didn't see anything in women other than an institution to be silently revered and protected. With affection, detachment, and an assumed superiority. Not you. You were a child when al-jidd died. Everyone else, in their own way, thought only of how to survive. You focused on something different: a mixture of resilience and peace. Under the mask, you had an acutely feminine sensitivity. Jidda was the person you sought refuge in when you couldn't be strong, when you needed an affection that didn't depend on your charm. Not the laughter that surrounded you when you were with friends, but the comfortable silence of not having to speak. With her you didn't mind losing at cards. You weren't worried about how you appeared—sure, you wanted to impress her, you wanted her to be proud of you, but for who you were, not what you did. She was always proud, since forever.

And you loved her in the same way. She was the best person you'd ever known, the opposite of what you admired in others: taciturn, isolated, sacrificed. No, maybe that's not how you saw her, maybe it's me judging her that way, because I can't stomach the idea of someone being happy in a life that's different from mine. It's difficult for those who create their own faith out of absolute freedom to admit that there are people who don't need to be saved from behind their own bars, and that maybe absolute freedom is its own invisible prison. Jidda cooked and worked, worked and cooked; she had no ambition other than to keep you all alive until you were old enough. She carried around with her all those she had lost, as if the ghosts clung to her ankles and kept her feet planted on the ground. When she moved from one room to another, every movement was reconciling and at the same time moving. She made peace with the ground through her bare feet, her dry heels. She moved something, something inside of you, as you watched her, and inside me now as I imagine her. You helped her set the table, wash the dishes; you sat next to her to listen to the singing during the holidays, you observed her as she closed her eyes and tapped the camel skin with her knotty fingers, and you didn't ask her what it meant.

You spent your life searching for the amused desperation that she carried, of a happy life lived in struggle.

For Liz, unhappiness is a defeat. She often remarks on the difficulty of someone's life, and her voice fills up with pity, as if to excuse some kind of failure. There's always a judgement in her benevolent gaze. So I too have learned to be ashamed of my life. But you didn't live like that, did you? Jidda didn't live like that. Have you ever lived a moment of happiness that wasn't also sad? Every thing contains its opposite.

3.

There was a guy, a white guy, who used to come and see you train. He would stand to one side with an expensive-looking camera and watch you. You pretended not to notice him and did everything you could to win. You didn't even know him, but you wanted him to not forget you. You wanted to say Look at me, I'm special, I'm a phenomenon. You never raised your eyes in his direction; the others ran over to him and talked to him, but you kept to yourself.

In the changing room, the other guys told you he was a sports agent. He had come from Berlin.

You speak German—Samir looked at you enviously—and you're the fastest in the four-hundred meters. He asked us about you, but you never go and speak to him.

A nonchalant smirk, as if you had better things to do. But your heart was beating like crazy.

You walked home with Idris trotting behind you. He had stolen a Walkman from a tourist, with a Jimi Hendrix cassette inside. He didn't stop listening to it all day. You were jealous, but you didn't want to give him the satisfaction of asking if you could listen. You thought obsessively about the German. How to attract him without making it obvious you wanted everything he could possibly give? How to charm him, how to amaze him? And then what would happen? You would go to Berlin. You would conquer Europe. In the mornings you'd go out and about with your own money in your pocket, looking in shop windows with the gaze of a man who could afford to step inside. You would live like a Westerner: you would have a girlfriend you didn't have to marry, just for fun. You'd take her to the cinema. Maybe you'd try würstel. The thought turned your stomach, but that too was added to the list of things that would make you free: doing what you wanted, and what you didn't, just because you could.

Idris tugged at your sleeve. You turned to look at him, distracted by your daydreams. He was holding out the battered earphones.

Do you want to listen?, he asked with his innocent smile. He too just wanted to be noticed. At the sound of Hendrix's guitar, your muscles melted. You felt your fingers start to pulsate. Nothing but the present existed: your brother's smile, the dust on your shoes, those scratchy noises that sounded like the true and dirty life you knew so well, your body moving. It was a strange thing, that music—it gave you permission to be angry, and sad, without anyone knowing.

Later that evening you polished your running shoes. They were the first sneakers you'd ever owned, and your brother Malik gave them to you. At that time, he was secretly going out with a girl called Karima who would become his wife and a thorn in the side of the rest of you who saw Malik like a father and her like a wicked stepmother. She was a gossip and liked to stick her nose in your business. She said that if you wanted running shoes you'd have to earn them for yourself; but Malik worked at the Post Office, brought home a fixed salary, and was distant but good. Distant but good was what you too learned to be. You didn't know what to say when he gave you the shoes. You were angry, because you felt indebted and because you were convinced that Malik had never loved you, that he preferred Idris, and that spontaneous act of generosity entrapped you in confused feelings: gratitude, fear of not deserving anyone's love, the wounded pride of still needing others. While cleaning the shoes, you imagined obtaining something for yourself that nobody would ever give you out of pity or brotherliness or a sense of responsibility, but only out of merit.

The next day you were nervous; you had never been nervous before. You had always been convinced you could win any competition without trying. You felt superior, and not because you thought the others were stupid or incompetent, but because you were convinced you were special, and that if you put the work in, you could do anything you wanted. When you saw the others get something, you found yourself desiring the same, whatever it was, especially if it was a talent. In a word, you were ambitious, but you didn't know what it meant, because you had been taught never to fully desire anything.

It was an average performance, not extraordinary. You knew that he had seen better, and you experienced it as an enormous failure. You decided to look over at him anyway: you wanted to be cocky and let him know that you didn't really care what he thought.

He smiled at you and beckoned you over; you looked away for a moment, wiping the sweat from your face with your t-shirt, to give yourself courage, play it cool. Finally you surrendered, walked over to him, and said hello in German. He didn't look surprised, which pleased you—he knew who you were.

You're good, he said quickly.

I can do better. You were scornful yet anxious to please him.

I'm sure you can, with the right training. Do you live near here?

Yes, two blocks away.

Were you born and brought up here?

Yes.

How many siblings do you have?

Five.

And your parents?

My mother is a dressmaker.

And your father?

He's no longer around. You shrugged.

I see.

He stood in silence for a while, then asked why you chose German rather than English.

Everyone does English.

And you're not everyone? He suggested with a hint of a smile. He had long, black hair, tied into a ponytail—this, and the delicate lines of his face, his light eyes, and his dark black eyelashes and eyebrows, gave him a very feminine look. It confused you.

No, you said resolutely, lowering your gaze. His hands were delicate too—well looked after, no callouses, clean.

You immediately hated him, but you were already promising yourself you'd take whatever he could give, so when he invited you to lunch you said yes, and you asked if your brother Idris could come too. He said yes, cold and kind at the same time.

You were hoping he'd take you to a place where rich people go, but instead you went to the bar near school. You were disappointed and relieved, prey to the contradiction of wanting something that also made you profoundly uneasy: money.

The bar had a small television. You spent hours in that room, drinking tea and playing chess for nothing but glory. You watched whatever was on the TV; sometimes they played French films with characters who smoked and drank wine from little round glasses. There was a profound distance between your world and the one represented in those films. That distance fascinated you. It was like a challenge. You had ferocious ambitions that you were ashamed to reveal. Ambition, like everything else, was mocked in the neighborhood. Tragedies of all kinds were laughed in the face of—anything that wasn't death hid a secret hilarity within. One time, a neighbor's gas tank exploded and he was hurled from the first floor balcony; it was a miracle he survived, but his whole face was toasted. In years to come, those who had been lucky enough to witness the scene told the story with tears in their eyes, holding a hand over the stitches in their stomachs from laughter. It was the funniest thing that had happened for a long time. I still remember your menacing laugh when you recounted these scenes to me; I was frightened by your relish for suffering. Your childhood seemed littered with errors committed in good faith, disguised as bad intentions. For some reason it was easier to accept them that way, easier to fake wickedness than confess naivety.

The waiter was one of Boubakar's old schoolmates. When he saw you sit down with that clean-cut white guy he understood immediately that this was a unique opportunity to wind you up. He approached your table, standing up straight, conducting himself like a dandy, and spoke in formal French, letting his Rs slip as if he were a maître d' at the Hôtel de Ville.

Idris immediately burst out laughing, then got kicked in the leg which broke his laughter into a whimper. He fell silent and hid his face in a yawn. You looked directly at the German, your head held high. You wanted him to know you weren't embarrassed, that you didn't feel inferior.

At the neighboring table there were two men in their sixties playing checkers and drinking coffee. They would remain silent for a long time but each time one of them made a move, the other burst into loud laughter, like a pair of hyenas. You got lost for a few minutes, your eyes stuck on their board. They weren't very good, or maybe they were trying to prolong the game.

The conversation continued and Idris, the German, and the waiter were now speaking in English, a language you didn't know. You were irritated: there was no way to get their attention that wouldn't seem childish. The German had brought you to lunch, you, he was interested in you, but suddenly you found yourself excluded from the game, you couldn't find a way in, just like you couldn't reach over to the next table and win someone else's game of checkers. Idris seemed perfectly at ease, which surprised you. That Walkman full of American music had trained his ear, he spoke English well and imitated the German's accent with ease. His ingenuousness made you laugh: the German, of course, had a German accent.

You waited a few minutes, then interrupted belligerently, speaking firmly in Moroccan: Bamou, bring us a taktuka, a zaaluk, and a chicken tagine. Then leave us be.

Bamou emitted a fat, catarrhous laugh full of smoke. What are you going to do with all that?

Idris shrugged, he loved being complicit. We're going to eat it.

Is he paying?

Obviously.

Yallah! And with his palms turned to you he lifted his hands to his chest as if to say: I surrender, lucky you someone is paying for your lunch while I'm here serving you.

You turned to the Kraut in an accomplished German: I've ordered for us all, I hope you don't mind.

He scrutinized you for a few seconds, then held his hand out across the table: We haven't introduced ourselves. I'm Karl, the athletics agent at the University of Berlin.

A shiver ran up your spine. You didn't say anything, but the tension accumulated on your neck, your forehead. It was hot, and you had the sensation that you were sticky, suddenly no longer hungry. You felt al-jidd's fingers on your neck.

You are good.

I can be better than what you saw. I was out of sorts. I can do better.

I know.

So?

Do you have plans for after high school?

You burst out laughing. Plans. What kind of plans could you possibly have? You happened to have been born in Derb Sultan: the plan was to survive. There weren't many roads to go down, and the ones you did have in your head, you didn't have the courage to share. The only feasible plan was to get work, find a respectable girlfriend, marry her, have two or three children, watch them grow up from a corner of the room without letting yourself get too close. Your children would grow up with the children of others, like the children of others. Your wife's cous-cous would never be jidda's cous-cous. You'd go to the bar every night. That was it: life.

But in the moment he asked that question and you burst out laughing, that life flashed before your eyes and you felt a fear that froze your blood. Your hands became rigid and the laughter died in your throat.

What have you got for me?, you asked, hiding behind the arrogance that only a scared teenager knows how to pull off.

A visa—he replied. You could come to Germany with a study visa and enter the athletics circuit. You're a bright boy, you run like a train, you know how to focus. And from what I've heard around, you're not someone who creates problems. You don't do drugs, you don't drink, you go shopping for your mother before school. Your grades are average but you can improve on them. If you wanted to, you could be brilliant. You could even get the grades to get a scholarship and come to Germany without having to pay for anything but the food you eat.

Idris's eyes were wide open. He had caught as much of the conversation as he needed. You felt repulsed and didn't know why. You were sitting there and you didn't know what to say, but more than anything else you no longer knew who you were, what to desire, what to pray for. Your Allah had dropped a perfect stranger into your hands and he was looking at you as if only he knew the things of the world and you felt, perhaps for the first time in your life—and it didn't happen many times afterward—inadequate.

You wanted to shake that insecurity off immediately, but it was clear that you couldn't afford the luxury of arrogance—you had to take it first; only later would you find out whether you wanted it or not. Secretly, piece by piece, you recomposed yourself, straightening your back, lifting your eyes, listening to the rhythm of your breath. Like a bolt of lightning, you saw your father opening the door of the house. Nothing more. Only the jangle of the keys, and the face of al-jidd in the half light of the doorway that opened directly into the living room, where the youngest were already sleeping, legs entangled, on the sofas that ran along the sides of the room. Only a thread of light entered through the window, but you observed him from under the covers—you were waiting for him, awake, like always, like thirty years later I would be too. When you heard the key in the lock you became immediately sleepy: Papà was home, and you were free to sleep. You weren't waiting up because you had something to ask him—he never responded to your questions, you couldn't run over to him, touch him, lay claim to his time—but because you were afraid that one of those nights you would remain awake, in vain, until morning, never to see him again. That night you were afraid of never came, because al-jidd died in the daytime and he died at home. But every night, since then, you waited up for him. Perhaps I'll stop sleeping now too.

Your father's face in the half light arose in your mind and you realized that he had been gone nearly ten years and that for nearly ten years you had slept only out of exhaustion, losing a silent battle against your eyelids every night. It's a thing you have carried with you your whole life: you forced Berta to have a TV in the bedroom and as she slept you lay there staring at the screen for hours and hours until your eyes burned.

You hadn't dreamed in almost ten years. You wondered if Idris would sleep when you were gone; you wondered if jidda would cry; you wondered who would protect your sister. Leaving is like dying in the hearts of those you leave behind.

Maybe that was the moment you understood that wanting or

not wanting is never an easy response, and that every granted wish requires a sacrifice. And yet you had to take that thing. As you watched Idris plunge into the tagine to carefully pick out the olives, you thought you could save everyone, take care of everyone.

I can study more, I can do better, you repeated. I can aspire to be better, I can dream of better, I can have better. Better than what? Better than the love of your mother? Better than the neighborhood? Better than laughter with your friends, better than the smell of meat on a Friday, better than mint tea? Better than the ocean, better than winning at cards, better than harira in winter? Much better. Better than the adhan, better than listening to the wolves howling at ammiti's house on the edge of the desert, with the stars a breath away from your nose, lying on the roof with Boubakar and Idris, you the only one awake, alone with the universe? Were you certain, Papà? That different is better, that more is better?

Karl took out a small notebook, scribbled something on it, then tore the page out and passed it to you. He had written his name, address, phone number, and a few other details. He told you to call him when you finished high school and fax him your grade report. You didn't know where to start looking for a fax machine, but you said nothing but yes, yes, yes, of course.

He looked at you strangely, the German. You could make 48 seconds, he said without irony.

I think I've already done it, once, you said, very serious.

He raised an eyebrow, suspicious. Really? In training or in a race?

You shook your head, holding in a smile. No, in the street. Some dogs were chasing me. You clumsily lifted up your knee and showed him the scars from the bites.

I had never run that fast before, you went on. But they got me all the same. A different kind of race, that one.

The German remained speechless for a minute, his gaze fixed on your leg, on which there were three white furrows where no hair grew. Finally, he shook his head, somewhere between amusement and resignation.

One is never running away from something, he said slowly; one only runs toward something.

That was when Idris spoke in English, in his timid but imperious tone: You can tell you've never been hungry. And he pierced Karl with eyes full of dignity. Idris had nurtured a secret rage, perhaps more ferocious than yours, because he was spoiled. Being spoiled and poor is a terrible combination. You can only want things you can't have.

Karl looked at you without resentment, but also without pity. As a young boy he had probably seen the war, had seen the horror, and you don't escape from that, no matter how fast you run. Perhaps that was what he meant, or perhaps it was just what he needed to believe.

No, he responded, perhaps not.

You wanted to change the subject, so you asked him to talk to you about Germany, about Berlin. There was a wall that divided the city into two opposite worlds. One had everything and the other had nothing; one was happy and the other sad, he said. He said that it was the Russians' fault.

Which side are you on?, you asked, curious.

He smiled and waved his hand as if to indicate a direction. The side you can get out from.

The two old men who were playing checkers had gone and you had exhausted your topics of conversation; you sipped your tea in silence. Karl looked at his watch and stretched. I must go, he said. He took out of his pocket a dark leather wallet that you looked at with immense envy; ran his finger over a stack of bank notes, and you instinctively grabbed him by the wrist and pushed his hand under the table. Never let people see your money, you said. Without turning around, you knew that almost everyone in the bar had noticed that he had a wad of bank notes in his pocket, a confirmation more than a surprise. Karl shrugged indifferently, put a dozen dirhams down on the table, then got up and slipped his wallet into the back pocket of his trousers.

Auf Wiedersehen, he said at the door of the bar with a smile. Be good!

You stared at door in silence as it closed behind him. It was Idris who stirred you with his raucous laugh; he was already angrily smoking cigarettes.

What's up?, you asked, irritated, squeezing between your fingers the piece of paper that one day, perhaps, would open the door to the world.

Idris raised a hand and showed you Karl's leather wallet.

You never saw that man again.

4.

It was summer and you were camping. You had taken the train to the north coast, near Melilla, with an enormous jamboree tent that jidda had sewn for you. You put it up on the beach and didn't move from there for the entire summer. You were there for a month or maybe two, until your food and money ran out. You had worked the whole year to save up for what you needed to survive. You took a gas stove on which you made Moroccan coffee for the boys in the mornings, adding black pepper powder. It was strong and spicy and stung your nose when you drank it. Smelling the intense aroma early in the morning while the others were still asleep, sitting on the sand looking out at the sea—small but precious things.

Before the coffee, at dawn, you ran. Running on the beach was a joy and a pain. Your feet sunk into the soft sand and made it harder, but the sun was rising up from the sea and the horizon becoming more defined, as gradually the blue of the sky and the water lightened and transformed. It was a timid light that gave you peace as you felt the cold salty air enter powerfully through your nose, your lungs exploding, your heart pushing insistently on your chest cavity as if making its way through a crowd. You loved how methodical running was, the comfort of knowing what happens next—but there was also the thrilling possibility of falling, tripping, injuring yourself. You could stop suddenly and dive into the water, or speed up and feel your body stretch out, expand, push away time. You thought of nothing but your breath; you couldn't be greedy with air, rather you savored it, felt it slowly reach your stomach, your knees, your calves, all the way down to your toes, and then slowly rise up again to your mouth. You treated your body like a channel of energy. It was your prayer. You used to say Allah was watching you when you ran.

You'd reach the little port and see the fishermen who, having unloaded their buckets full of every type of fish onto the beach, brought the boats in under a canopy. You helped them pull the boats up and tie them with ropes so they wouldn't slip back into the sea. You knew the knots—you'd been taught by other fishermen on other beaches, always at dawn. The men, tired, didn't refuse your help even though they knew they couldn't pay you. In the end they'd put a few live fish in a bag, still thrashing around, and gift them to you. You'd return to the tent with your feet in the water. It was freezing first thing in the morning; it tickled your ankles.

You thought of nothing.

You dug a hole on the wet beach, in the shade, and put the bag of fish into it. Then you made the coffee.

You were close to the small city of Melilla, a Spanish enclave. You needed a visa to get in and Samir was the only one who had one, so he could go and do the shopping once a week. One morning he returned with a bag of crisp pears. He took one, cut it into small pieces and gave you each a morsel. You looked at him as if he had grown a second head.

Are you joking?

No—if we just eat one a day they'll last us the rest of the holiday.

Samir was authoritative: he was older and he had a deep, manly voice. You looked at him with irritation but said nothing. You ate your morsel of pear slowly.

That night, lying in the tent, you listened to the concert of breathing. You were hungry. You hated Samir, so sure in his role as leader, the skill he had in maintaining control over when you could have a drop of sugar and how much; in perpetrating his power, day in, day out, in granting you each your piece, at his discretion. You hated him because he had been cunning and you had never thought of doing the same with your fish—you had never taken advantage of the others' hunger. For some reason, though, the sense of moral superiority did not console you in the slightest: you poured out the coffee and served up the fish, and not bestowing importance on either thing simply meant they didn't have it. Samir, on the other hand, treated those stupid pears like jewels in a crown, so that's what they became, and you of course wanted a crown, for the sole reason that he had it and you didn't.

You felt the bite of hunger. You had eaten tinned beans the night before and the smell in the tent was unbearable. Idris was snoring next to you. Your stomach grumbled and you stopped yourself from letting out air, fearful that someone was awake and would hear. You thought of the German and your moment, which felt further away each day. You thought of the man you would be able to become, of all the things you would do when you had the money. You wanted to become extremely rich and buy a million pears.

In the meantime, however, there was a bag of them just outside the tent and they were free. A bite, just one, wouldn't do any harm. Maybe just a slap from Samir, but you could take it. There's a certain dignity in paying the fine without complaint. One bite. *Crack!* Like stepping on a dry twig. You held it in your mouth, partly to make it last longer, partly to soften it so that it would be less noisy when you chewed. You sucked the sugar, and the water pooled under your tongue.

You took another bite.

When the others woke up the next morning, the bag of pears was no longer there. Idris looked at you, a jolt of comprehension in his eyes. He said nothing but scratched his nose with his thumb to hide a satisfied sneer—it was as if he had eaten them, because he was your brother. Your stomach was also his.

Where are the pears? Samir was digging around in the sand like a dog. He turned frenetically to look at you all and he looked like a little boy, just like the rest of you, a child whose chocolate had been stolen. That bag had elevated him, made him in some way the father of you all. You all wanted to be fathers to the others, perhaps because none of you knew how to be a son.

You were ready to take a serious beating. You didn't deny it even for a second. There's no shame in being hungry: it's the earthliest experience there is. Hunger is everything. It's everything you want and everything you have. It unifies the inside with the outside.

You said: I ate them, and your chest deflated like a balloon at the end of a party. I'm sorry, I couldn't sleep, I couldn't think of anything else, I couldn't stop myself.

There was a moment of silence in which you beat yourself up in guilt: you had eaten the pears but you had nothing to give in exchange. You were in debt. You looked at your feet like a servant. You wanted to pay the price and stop feeling so mortified. And instead, the silence pressed down on you like a heel on your neck, and your breath stopped.

You hated, hated, hated to be in the wrong.

The strange thing was that, when you finally looked up, you saw them smiling, almost giggling. You didn't understand what was happening.

What is it? Was there something in the pears? Instinctively you put a hand on your stomach to check it wasn't about to explode.

It was Samir who responded: I thought about doing it too. I dreamed about eating them—you know when you're half-asleep and you want to do something but you just can't get up because of the sleep. I would have done it if I'd woken up, and he waved his hands in the air, as if to express a frustration toward himself rather than you. The point wasn't that you had eaten the pears, but that you'd got there before him. Everything was a race. Even a betrayal.

Me too, I was also almost there, about to get up . . . said another brother, and then another. Idris put a hand on your shoulder and whispered: I'm glad I didn't wake up, because it meant that you didn't have to share them with anyone.

Maybe at that point you'd have liked to find the courage to tell him that you would have willingly shared them with him because you loved him, that he was the only reason you hadn't left yet: you wanted to make sure he would cope, that he wouldn't throw his life to the dogs without you. Nobody else would look out for him; it was you who had to bring him up, to protect him. He was your little brother, you didn't have another and you wouldn't find another in Europe.

5.

It wasn't that you'd completely given up on the idea of leaving, just that something always got in the way. You didn't want to leave jidda, who was always crying in those days because Zahra had gotten herself into trouble. She had married the first stranger who was kind to her—but she got it wrong, he wasn't a kind man. It was yours and your brothers' fault, of course: you had never given her much attention, so she'd got it into her head that she didn't deserve much, and that she should move out as soon as she could. Maybe it wasn't conscious, but you were all mean to her: she scared you; she wore her heart like an overcoat, outside rather than in, and used it to protect herself rather than protecting it. You boys who used to tease her and laugh at all the feelings she had now didn't know how to manage a pain that was irrefutable even to your eyes: you felt terrified and inadequate confronting her exhausted face, after another sleepless night staring at the door hoping it would remain closed. But every night he came back.

They had married a year earlier. He had come to the house with his parents and told you he wanted her, "your" Zahra. He had seen her shopping at the market, buying fabrics, and then at the entrance to the hammam. They had chatted. He wasn't one of your friends but he was from the neighborhood. You knew him by sight: he seemed polite, from a good family, modest, educated, similar to you in the ways that mattered. At that time Zahra was working as a seamstress with jidda, but the money wasn't enough for both of them and she knew, as everyone did, that she needed to be independent as soon as possible, so as not to be a burden on Malik, who was now married and had young children and couldn't provide for everyone forever.

So you gave Zahra away to a stranger, one could say. But it's not entirely true. The fact is that Zahra herself thought she was in love with this man who had been kind to her, and that was enough for you, because the rest could be built, could be learned. You can learn to love regardless of the person, you learn it like you learn a trade. With no expectations, with modesty, with dedication.

It's hard to admit when you've done harm to someone you love. At that time Zahra didn't have many people to talk to, and she certainly didn't have you. You were angry with everything; you felt trapped and thought only of yourself, convinced that being physically present for jidda and the others was a sufficient sacrifice and that you could keep your brain, at least, for yourself.

She was alone, and you didn't care. When, one afternoon a month after the wedding, you thought you were alone in the house and you heard her sobs, you didn't have a clue how to start worrying.

You walked into the kitchen like normal.

What are you doing here?

Maman is at Malik's house; Karima has the flu so she can't look after the children. Someone needs to look after you guys.

No one told me.

Well now they have.

She was bent over the hob, moving quickly between the jars of spices and the old fridge, which you had to kick closed as it was always hanging half open. You couldn't catch her expression; you noticed she wasn't wearing her hijab and her face was hidden by her hair, but there was something else strange in her tone and in her shoulders, which were rigid as if the invisible wire that held her together and attached to the ground was wedged between her shoulder blades. You observed the way she twitched like a frightened animal and suddenly a thought flitted through your head. You reached out an arm, grabbed her wrist and turned it toward you. She jolted back and knocked the pan on the fire, splattering boiling water everywhere. She shouted, she was scared—of the water, of you, of the world.

Zahra, calm down, what are you doing?

Don't touch me! Her whole body was trembling. Don't touch me, I said don't touch me!

But what's happened? You were afraid, now. You had never heard a woman raise her voice in anger.

You moved closer again, slowly, and tried to pull her toward you. She exploded into a slow and painful whining, wheezing.

Zahra, can you tell me what's happened to you?

You held her by the shoulders and tried to look at her face. Your heart leapt into your throat, you had pins and needles in your hands, Zahra was crying even louder now, your body was numb.

After a while she started to wriggle out of your hold, turned back to the hob, sniffing powerfully. But you stayed there, immobile, looking at the swollen face of your sister.

A few minutes passed before one of you found the strength to speak. Zahra pushed you over to the table, sweetly, with a hand on your shoulder but without arrogance. She put a cup of mint tea down in front of you, and its fresh smell stirred you for a moment.

Was it Khaled?

Omar. There's no use talking about it.

He hit you. Do you know what Boubakar will do as soon as he sees you? He'll either kill him or kill himself. I don't know which, but I'm sure he'll do one.

And what good will that do for me? It certainly won't buy me a new face.

You'd never heard her talk like this, more tough than fragile, more angry than pained.

He is still my husband. I chose him, I wanted him. What is it maman says?

You can't cry if you are the cause of the pain, you responded instinctively. You watched her sip her tea with all the dignity that women have when they suffer. Her bruised left eye, her split and swollen lower lip. She was composed in that moment, her body seemed to float elegantly in the air. You looked at her as if it was the first time, thinking how much she looked like jidda, more than all of you. Only now did you recognize that the slow movements of jidda, the tenderness of her gestures, her wistful, silent eyes—all of the things, essentially, that you mistook for a sweetness that was devoted to you, of which you were the cause and the effect—weren't sweetness. She was sad, jidda. Proud and sad.

We need to do something, you murmured, and you felt like a child under her resigned gaze. It can't go on like this.

I just need to be more careful, she said blowing on her tea, her lips tight.

Of what?

Of not speaking when not asked.

Of not speaking . . . ?

Omar, you don't understand: out there it's not like it is in our house. We were brought up with just maman. She has always been the center of our world, but that's not normal. Have you ever asked your friends how they treat their women? I mean, ultimately, how you treat me? Let me tell you: you ignore me. I don't exist for anyone apart from maman, and now for Khaled. But I have to cut off my tongue, because when he gets home he doesn't want to hear about me, he just wants to eat. And after eating he wants to rest, and after that we go to sleep. It's the next morning, when his breath is heavy and I am still sleeping, that I exist for him. In the evening it's as if the dishes fly onto the table by themselves. But in the morning, all of a sudden his hands are all over me, and it often seems like there are more than two of them . . . But I have to stay quiet, you see, because nothing good will come of speaking.

I knew that marrying him was a bad idea. You didn't even know him!

She stayed silent for a minute, then she asked: Do you know how old I am?

You didn't know.

Twenty-six, Omar. At twenty-six maman had already brought half of our family into the world. I don't know how to tell you that my destiny in this life is not to do what I want. I understand that it's difficult for you to get your head around that, because it's the only thing you think about, day and night: what you want, how to obtain it, how to leave everyone behind and still sleep soundly at night. I don't have that luxury: I have never asked myself what I want. But I do know what I don't want: I don't want to be a burden to maman. I don't want to find myself alone and without children with the neighbors looking at me and saying "poor thing." Nobody is a poor thing here, because we are all poor, yet nobody laughs with me and they look at me with pity. I don't want to be the only soul in Derb Sultan to have to endure people's pity.

Zahra, nobody pities you. It's just that we don't know what to say, because you're so different from us.

I wouldn't be so different from you if you'd taken me to the bar with you every now and then . . .

But you can't come to the bar with us, you know that. It wasn't me who made the rules, it's just the situation: you're a woman.

Omar, do you think I'm beautiful?

She latched onto your gaze with the dark stare of a demon; she forced you to properly weigh her question. Beautiful wasn't the word you would have used to describe Zahra. She hadn't been carefree enough to be beautiful—for you, at that time, beauty meant having a lightness in your eyes. The truth is that Zahra was born tired. She had a tired body, crumpled in on itself—her face, her gestures, everything in her seemed to express a sense of subdued resignation to time passing, as if she endured the days rather than living them. Perhaps it was you boys who put all that tiredness onto her, relegating her to forming the background of your existence, to listening to your adventures without ever taking part, to being the eternal spectator of family life, never the protagonist.

Do people exist if nobody sees them?

Without waiting for your response, Zahra burst out laughing. Do you see my problem? You had to think about it, maybe because you've never looked at me before. Khaled noticed me. Out of all the women, he noticed me. Do you know something? My expectations of what I deserved were extraordinarily low. Do you know what I prayed for, morning and night, when I was little? I didn't ask Allah to bring baba back. I didn't ask for us to be rich. I asked for one thing, five times a day, every day.

What?

To make me a boy.

6.

Over the months that followed, as you pondered your next move, Zahra began to put on weight. Boubakar didn't go near her because she had a spirit in her belly. Khaled no longer went near her either, which was for the best. She walked around the neighborhood now with her head held high: she had won her battle; she would never be lonely again. Her skin glowed and her body finally seemed rooted in the earth like something magnificent and divine. She no longer needed to justify her presence; she belonged to every room—apart from the one where the men smoked and drank tea. Men's tea was different from women's tea: it was prepared separately in a specific teapot that the women weren't to touch. It was infused for longer, with very little sugar and more tea than mint.

Zahra's belly, overnight, had corrected a series of things. Malik and Karima, who usually kept to themselves, started coming back to the neighborhood, and jidda seemed twenty years younger, behaving as if Zahra were a little girl again, pampering her all the time. Zahra had begun to sleep at jidda's house, because Khaled was a light sleeper and couldn't stand being woken up every time she went to the bathroom. You and Idris suspected that Khaled just couldn't stand Zahra, full stop; in his eyes she had completed her obligations as a wife. This consoled you for a while, but you started to see him more and more often at the bar, his eyes red, his frown surly. He would greet you with just a nod of the head, not like family.

In the meantime, things happened around you of which you

saw only the effects. Morocco had gone to war with Algeria over the annexed territories of the Western Sahara. Nobody in the neighborhood left, but you suffered the hunger of war: in those months the price of flour doubled and nobody could buy bread anymore. People became nervous.

It was June 20, 1981. You, Boubakar, and Idris were at the bar with Samir. You were playing chess. For a few days you had been forced to buy everything on credit. In the mornings you'd go to the bar and order tea, drink half the pot, and save the rest for the afternoon. The owner, behind the counter, would heat it up for you without saying anything: you weren't the only ones, if he hadn't done you that favor maybe you wouldn't have come back the next day, and he couldn't afford to take that risk.

Boubakar had nothing to smoke and was intractable; he spent the day swearing incessantly under his breath.

Shit!, you exclaimed when Samir, sniggering, put you in checkmate. I can't think on an empty stomach!

Friend, we are all on an empty stomach. Ah! You never lose at chess! I wish there were more people here to witness my victory. It's the only good thing that's happened to me this week . . .

Boubakar snarled some insults through his teeth that were directed at King Hassan II and nobody contradicted him. By that point you never left the neighborhood, you were all too tired and angry. Silence fell. Samir nervously drummed his fingers on the table. Nobody could think of anything to say or do that would distract them from the hunger. You didn't like the atmosphere; you felt defenseless and impotent.

Do you remember when we used to go to the game?, you blurted out, just for something to say.

Idris raised his eyes to the ceiling, exasperated: The stupid story of how you used to swindle the guys at the stadium? You've already told it a million times, it's not even that funny.

It just annoys you because we never let you come with us,

you replied with a hint of a smile. He looked at you resentfully, and for a few seconds he was a child again. Boubakar burst out laughing, nostalgic for those times in which Idris was a chubby little cherub and everyone's thoughts were light and fluctuated without fanfare, coming and going of their own accord, leaving no trace.

You knew a guy who had a little kiosk at the stadium where he sold sandwiches, fries, and other American things during the match. You would go there in the morning and help him unload the goods. He'd then hide you in a small room in the stadium and you'd remain there, squatting, for hours, until the place was quiet again. Then one of you would creep out, place a plastic sheet with a sign saying "RESERVED" over a dozen seats in the stands, and then go back to the room to hide. When people began to arrive, you'd come out and disperse into the crowd. Each of you sat down separately, as if you didn't know one another. Then Samir, who was the most brazen one, would come out of the stadium and sell the "reserved" seats for triple the ticket price.

He didn't care at all for the game, he just liked playing the system, and he liked money. That money in his pocket was the certainty that, whatever happened, he would go to bed with a full stomach that night. And that, for some of you, was not a given. He knew this better than anyone else and, even if he did the most dangerous bit of the scam, he would split the gains evenly with all of you, who had watched the match without lifting a finger. For some time afterward, you thought about it every time you walked past his house.

How good were those sandwiches we made after the match, whispered Samir, stretching his arms up in a yawn. He looked like an angry cat.

And the popcorn! Boubakar exclaimed. We even got a Coke!

Suddenly the owner of the bar, an old man called Jamal who

had watched you grow up, came over looking conspiratorial. You all immediately fell silent, because he was an elder and, where you were from, elders demanded respect above all else. He looked at you from under his bushy eyebrows with his black eyes: Do you know what's happening tomorrow?, he whispered.

You shook your heads, confused.

The revolution, he continued in a very low voice, bending over you like an old willow, his long beard caressing the scraggy chest under his light tunic.

The revolution?

The revolution. Against the king.

Alhamdulillah! Boubakar exclaimed, his eyes open wide.

Shhh! Jamal quieted him, looking surly. That big mouth of yours will get us all killed. Then he bent even deeper over you: Tomorrow at midday, be in front of the old court house. He gripped your shoulder, tight, his knuckles white. You nodded seriously.

The next day, your lives changed.

7.

At the beginning, there were few of them. Some boys had bars in their hands, others rocks. Poor people's weapons, children's weapons. They had told you it would begin in the north but that you should be ready. You all thought you were; you thought you were there for a reason. You thought you were there to get justice. But the truth is you weren't interested in justice, you weren't even interested in bread. You were just angry.

Angry because you were born here and not there. Angry because you were good at everything you did and it came to nothing. Angry because you sang at weddings but couldn't study music, because you ran like the wind but couldn't escape poverty. Angry because you felt like you were suffocating, at night, sleeping among all those hot, noisy, annoying, cumbersome bodies. They were your brothers, but you didn't know them and they didn't know you. Yet people confused you and you felt that nobody, nobody, perhaps not even jidda, really saw the differences between you. Boubakar had an icy stare, Samir was capable of memorizing all the cards in poker, Zahra stayed awake all night staring at the ceiling because she was afraid of the man who snored next to her—nobody gave a shit. Lose one child, lose them all. You were interchangeable. You couldn't stand how your edges were frayed. Your voice was deeper than Idris's, firmer than Boubakar's. Your hands were big, wrapped tightly around a rock, your nails flat. You were listening to your breath. You felt the earth pulsate. The city shook.

* * *

They arrived from the city center together, the guerrillas and the police. A mush of blood and noise. A boy you didn't recognize straight away, the younger brother of someone from the neighborhood, ran toward you, his face dirty, and told you they were coming round the corner, that they had jeeps, pistols, and tear gas. You looked at Samir; you were scared but you couldn't say it. Something in his eyes scared you even more: they were gleaming. He was so excited, almost ecstatic. He looked like he'd been waiting his whole life for the moment that he could finally square up all the injustice he had endured; for having dropped out of school at sixteen, for having to work in some shitty store when he had a brain that could've done anything; he could've been an engineer, a mathematician, a con artist. It's dangerous, you found out later, to be aware of your own unexpressed potential. We tend to idealize the lives not lived and hate the only one that counts: the life we have. It eats away at you from the inside.

Samir was a ticking time bomb. You looked down and saw his white knuckles gripping a rock so tightly they bled. You wanted to say something. Something you would have wanted someone else to say to you: Run. Leave it. Go home and lock the door. Think of your mother. There are other ways. Don't take the risk. You're still young.

But you said nothing. Because your lives, in that moment, didn't matter to you. You were ready to throw everything to the dogs.

You all started to run, first compact like a Roman squadron, then with less certainty. You and Samir stayed close. Out of the corner of your eye, you saw Idris dragging Boubakar. You felt relief, and envy. You and Samir had a plan, you had always had a plan: you were going to grow old together in Europe.

You heard the shots. The police appeared around the corner

like a flock of swallows, all dressed in black. The jeeps were right behind them. They fired shots everywhere: at you, at storefront windows, at the windows of houses, at you, at the sky, at the street lamps, at the railings, at the earth, at the too-big children, at you, at the old people with fragile bodies, at the signs, at the fruit carts, at the doors, at the roofs, at you.

Once you'd thrown your rocks there wasn't much more you could do. You suddenly saw that you were stupid, and that up until that point you'd understood nothing about life. That your ego would do you nothing but harm, that you were not special, and that if there was one thing that Allah had given you it was your fast legs. Only he hadn't given them to you so you could win something, or to conquer Berlin, but to save your life in that precise moment. Everything would begin and end in that one act of survival, of loving attachment to life.

Everything around you was chaos. They had fired tear gas. You grasped at the air like a blind man in the hope of finding Samir again and dragging him away with you. But you gave up after a few seconds. He who looks back dies, you thought. You started to run in a diagonal line; you ran backwards, you ran bent over, you ran crawling, all to not lose them from sight and to find an escape route. You slipped down a side street, you knew that a jeep wouldn't fit down there, but there were men on foot, and you thought they would take you one by one.

You ran like a man who was afraid of dying. You started shouting like a madman, running and knocking on doors that nobody opened, your nose was dripping, your vision was foggy, you thought of jidda who didn't deserve another dead son. Finally you found a half-open door and slipped inside, ran up the stairs, heard sounds at your back but didn't turn around, there was a sunny terrace, no corner in which to hide in those low neighborhood houses, they would see you from the street. A couple of meters down there was another terrace. You jumped. Your ears were ringing, at your back all kinds of noises, broken windows, shouts, shots. You went into an apartment building, another flight of stairs led to a room that was warm like a sauna.

What are you doing here?, an old lady asked. She was sitting on a mattress laid out on the floor and she held two needles in her hands; she was knitting.

If they find me they'll kill me, you told her. Then you wiped your face with your t-shirt, ashamed of the way your voice cracked. She had the body of a little girl; she looked so fragile. Everything looked, to you, on the point of breaking, folding in on itself: the crumbling walls of the poky room, the empty teacups on the tray resting on the floor, the sky that came in through the open window, her, her porous bones, your clumsy, too-big body. If they find me they'll kill me, you repeated. You were so tired you couldn't even dry your tears.

The old woman got up, staggering, which felt like it took a lifetime. She pointed, without words, at the mattress. You looked at her, speechless, but she pointed at it again with an impatient look in her eyes. You crawled under it, flattening yourself like a cockroach. You felt her sit down on top of you and arrange the blankets to cover the protuberance of your body.

After a few minutes they arrived.

Has anyone come in here? One of the two policemen asked her in an unfriendly voice.

I've not seen anything—she said, not hesitating, her tone bitter—but I can hear the inferno coming from the street. Gunshots at prayer time. What kind of Muslims are you? Can we not even pray in peace in this city?

You didn't know what the agent's face looked like, how they were looking at one another. You held your breath, all the muscles in your body contracted in the effort to make yourself tiny.

You felt his footsteps come closer, looking around.

If you see something, you call us.

She moved, sinking into the mattress, squashing you under

her weight. I shan't be calling anyone, she said laconically. Violence doesn't please Allah, nor me.

You heard the agent mutter something, then his heavy boots walking away. You remained under that mattress for what felt like hours, in silence, squashed by the body of the old woman without a name who had just saved your life. It was the second time a stranger had changed the course of your life. You wondered if free will truly existed, if the reason for your being so angry was that you hadn't followed the breadcrumbs Allah had laid out for you, to allow you to do what you had to do in this life. You thought of the German, and of how you had let that opportunity slip away out of pure cowardice, out of fear of failing. Now Allah had saved you again, and this time you had to be grateful and follow his word. Run, he was saying. Get as far from this neighborhood as you can.

At that point the old woman moved, you felt her weight lighten and your lungs filled with relief. You didn't move. Would you like some tea?, she whispered, lifting one edge of the mattress with a smile. It was dark outside. Everywhere hurt.

You drank the tea in silence.

What was happening down there? She asked, looking at you furtively from behind the cup that she held with both hands.

People dying of hunger, people dying of guns . . . you shrugged.

People surviving, she concluded, as if wanting to bring you both back down to earth.

Neither of you said anything else. After finishing your tea, you walked over to her, kissed the palm and the back of each of her hands, like you did with your mother. You looked around a final time: that poky room felt like a palace, and she a queen, because you were alive.

You returned home in the dark, the remnants of the fighting under your feet. Bewildered, you observed the disorder you had created—part of you wondered if it had all been a nightmare. You couldn't make sense of the fact that it had really happened: the shots, the revolt, the batons, the gas. You didn't know where your brothers were, and they didn't know where you were. Your legs, exhausted, seamlessly followed your thoughts, and you found yourself running again. The door of the house was open, you ran up the stairs two at a time, you threw open the door and found everyone there: jidda, Zahra, Idris, Boubakar, even Malik and his wife Karima. You didn't understand anything anymore. You had made jidda cry, your big brothers were looking at you almost with irritation, you felt stupid for having worried everyone. Then your gaze met Idris's. He was clearly convinced you had died—black puddles in the place of his eyes, as if he had lost all peace—and you hugged him. It was the first time since al-jidd's funeral, when you had held him to you because he was all that you had. That was still true.

For a moment you felt happy to be home; even when, a few seconds later, Malik beat you up. You could have defended yourself, but you received his punches almost with gratitude. They made you feel alive.

We have to go to the Khadars' house, Malik said once you'd finished and recomposed yourselves. The others nodded and you looked at them confused: To Samir's? Where? Why?

That was when you noticed a hole the size of a bullet in the window. Around the hole was a web of cracks.

Ensnared in that web were the memories of a friend who you played rummy with in the slow hours, who you raced against for everything, whom you'd dreamed of a different life alongside.

Samir would never see Europe.

8.

After you had all torn your clothes in grief, after days spent stifling your rage, dozens to a room, sobbing rivers of prayer, expelling the sense of injustice, hosting death in your dreams, greeting her on waking, seeing her in the extinguished eyes of the people at the bar who had stopped playing. After all of this, in the evenings, when the sun was low in the sky, you, Idris, and Boubakar sought refuge on the playing field in the middle of the running track. You smoked the little weed that was left, hardly talking. Idris detested this atmosphere. He had grown up with grief in his heart and now seeing that same void all around scared him. He was usually angry, like most young men, but obliging. Now it seemed that nothing could placate him. Even sitting still, he trembled. He had a nervous tic in his leg and in the silence he continually cleared his throat, as if trying to liberate a lump that wouldn't come up or go down.

You were working full time at the store. You wanted to make a bit more money so you could give some to Samir's family; you put aside everything you could, even though you were earning peanuts. At night you lay wide awake, turning between your fingers an old piece of paper with the phone number of a German man whose name you no longer remembered. Years had passed since then, and it felt like further years had passed since the bread riots. You no longer felt special—you no longer felt much at all. Your brain was foggy, and sometimes you felt you weren't present in your body but watching reality from the outside, like the ghost of one of your dead brothers. When you did feel alive, you wanted not to be: you felt new feelings that scared you because you didn't know what to call them. You were full of a quiet, eviscerating well of sadness; a dull sense of guilt for the mere fact of breathing; and, more than anything else, the nostalgic surrender of the elderly, who look back with misty eyes and accept that the hour has come to shuffle off this mortal coil, because they have experienced all that there is to experience in this life.

You are too young for the face you wear, jidda repeated. For the first time you made no effort to play the part of the superhero for her. You no longer cared about impressing her, amazing her, consoling her. You had nothing to show, not because you had arrived, but because you no longer knew which way you were going.

Zahra was there, ready to give birth to her daughter. She moved slowly, her belly the size of a watermelon, and she hadn't left the house since the day of the revolt. Everything frightened her, especially Khaled. When he came to visit, she would curl up in the chair with her eyes cast downward, almost as if she were in front of the king. You watched them—he gorging himself on food, she looking at the floor, her hands nervously over her stomach—and you suspected that it wasn't going to end well.

You no longer prayed. You couldn't find the energy and comfort you felt before, as if you were truly talking to someone. You stopped going to the mosque, which broke jidda's heart. She never said it to you, but you knew it made her suffer. You were angry with Allah: for twenty years you had turned to him, day after day, as if to the father you didn't have. You told him everything, asked him to protect you, to give you strength. Your faith wasn't a communal thing. No, it was an intimate thing, yours and only yours, one of the few things you didn't feel you had to share with anyone. Like with jidda, you felt you had a special relationship with Allah. After Samir's death you could no longer feel special: you were just one of the many who had gotten lucky while others hadn't. The randomness of death was the main source of your anguish; it pulverized you. There was no reason for which you went right and he went left. And if death can come like that, out of nowhere in any moment, what meaning is there for the suffering and ambition, the perseverance, the patience? Patience for what?

You spoke of this often with Boubakar and Idris, smoking on the stands around the running track, from where, years earlier, the German had watched you.

You've got it all wrong, little brother, said Boubakar one evening, slowly exhaling smoke. He was wearing a dark green skullcap and round glasses. He looked like a Moroccan John Lennon. You're waiting for who knows what from life, you're waiting and waiting and waiting for the day that you'll do something or have something. But life isn't doing and having, is it? You don't do, you don't have—you just are. And as long as you are, you should focus on being happy, not special. What's the point in being special?

I don't know, you responded, with a strange lump in your throat.

It's like with music, Idris said quietly. In the end it doesn't matter where you are or how much money you have. Even if you were rich, you'd be listening to Hendrix with the same ears.

All meat is the same, and it's all good, continued Boubakar.

All meat isn't the same, you rebutted, some cuts cost more than others. Wouldn't you like to eat the best meat in the world?

Boubakar shrugged. Whatever the cut, if you cook it enough it'll melt in your mouth. You don't need money, little brother—it's patience you need.

9.

Then, one evening, Zahra shouted out in the silence. The little girl was arriving. Jidda, who had borne many children, prepared the lukewarm water, the white sheets, the towels. The women of the neighborhood came together. There was endless coming and going. The men sat in a room with the door closed drinking tea. Even Boubakar avoided meddling. But you and Idris sneaked in, because you had learned to admire this crying sister who was about to do something miraculous and awesome and you boys, with twenty years under your belts, felt like children again in the presence of this mystery.

Zahra wouldn't have it.

Take me to the hospital, she hissed through her teeth. She was gripping your mother in terror: Nobody can die today, maman.

Jidda's face was extremely pale.

I beg you, Zahra wheezed, crying hot tears. It's a girl, maman. A little girl. I pray.

Who knows if it was that final sentence that broke jidda's indecision. A girl must be protected immediately, from the first moment. Or perhaps it's that we just can't afford to lose a girl because she'll be all we have when those men in the other room leave us to ourselves.

You ran into the men's room: Khaled, do you have your car? We need to take her to the hospital.

Khaled looked at you in irritation: What are you, the messenger of womankind?

Silence fell.

He, as always, was the first to look away. Why the hospital? There are twenty women here ready to help her, he muttered, drumming his fingers on the side of his teacup.

You turned to Malik, who had already stood up and was rummaging in his pockets. He nodded at you, his gaze firm, then raised the corner of his left eyebrow in that way that only you brothers could do. His tacit advice was that it wasn't worth it. You started toward the door without saying anything more, and the events that followed happened very quickly. Out of the corner of your eye you saw Idris move behind you. Dog-like grunts and the unmistakable cracking of a breaking nose.

There's some frozen meat in the kitchen, you mumbled. Boubakar chuckled, passing in front of you with his hands waving in the air, lungs shaken into a scratching song of gratitude. The women clapped their hands, children rolled around on the floor, all the doors in the building were open and preparations were in full swing. The smell of mint, cumin, meat, and sweat. Zahra was crying, there was blood on Idris's hand but maybe it was from the meat, there was the third to last cushion from the sofa that had visible stitching in the corner, a white thread, you pulled at it with your teeth. Inside was your money, you grabbed it all, jidda didn't like going in the car. Zahra asked: Where's Khaled? Boubakar squeezed her hand while continuing to sing, you too sang, you had the voice of a child, high and faltering. In the waiting room the smoke gathered beneath the low ceiling, the cold neon lights intermittently extinguished, it felt like a dream, jidda even asked Boubakar for a cigarette. Women never smoked in public. But many are the things women didn't do that jidda did.

Now Zahra was alone, alone with Allah. You touched the money in your pocket.

Inshallah, inshallah.

Hours passed, then they came and said to jidda that she could enter. Only her. You approached the doctor and asked how much was owed, but he smiled. This is a public hospital, dear boy, you don't pay. You wondered why you hadn't been brought here when the dogs took half your leg off, or the time your aunt's donkey hurled you off its back and onto a prickly pear. They'd taken the spines out using chewing gum. Free, eh? You burst out laughing. May Allah bless you!, you exclaimed, drying your tears. You, Malik, Idris, and Boubakar returned home to get Khaled.

You found the house full of people dressed in white; someone had summoned the entire neighborhood. There were people playing and singing your Berber songs. The neighbors, and the neighbors' neighbors, and their children. Khaled wasn't there. He was nowhere to be seen.

Malik took you to one side, his face darkened. For a moment he reminded you of your father: I tried to stop him, to make him see sense, but he made a run for it. He's a good for nothing, but he's her husband. What do we say to people?

This was what concerned the brother who had his life sorted out, who no longer came to visit jidda because his wife was repulsed by the rats of Derb Sultan. You and the rats were all made of the same dough, even Malik. Survivors. But he pretended he'd been born again the day he started working at the Post Office.

We'll tell them the truth, that he didn't deserve our sister. Better that way—you cut him short without looking at him. You felt again the rage that made your blood boil, feverish.

Omar, be serious. Who's going to look after the three of them now?

You loved Malik. You loved him because he had given you your first running shoes, and you knew he wasn't as stingy as he made out. He was just selfish and ungrateful. That night you did nothing but bite your tongue; you were incubating a decision that no longer needed words.

You still had the money in your pocket.
I'll take care of them.
How?
Leave it to me. Don't worry.

Boubakar and Idris were sitting on the sidewalk outside the house. For some reason, in that moment they couldn't muster happiness. They sensed, each in their own way, that everything had just changed.

You're leaving, said Idris all of a sudden. It wasn't a question.

Yes, you responded.

Boubakar nodded. He was lucid for once and seemed bigger than you: I know a guy at the port. I can get you onto a boat for Tangier, then you can figure it out from there.

You wanted to say many things, but you felt a knot in your throat that wouldn't go up or down. They must have felt the same, because you all remained silent for a long time.

When? Asked Idris, bluntly.

I'll wait to see the girl, you responded without thinking. For years you had been postponing, postponing, postponing.

Yeah, giggled Boubakar. Then you'll wait to see her first birthday. And then for maman to stop crying. And then for Idris to find a decent job. And then for . . . for me to stop smoking! He laughed, and he cried from laughter, or maybe it wasn't that.

You went home. Nobody noticed you, you felt invisible, as if Allah had put a spell on you. You put all your belongings into an old duffle bag that might have belonged to your father. You wanted to think so in that moment, to give you strength. You put the photo of al-jidd under Idris's Walkman, along with a bit of money. Jidda's copy of the Qur'an. You took a hawawashi from the fridge for the road. And your running shoes, which you hadn't used for months, not since Samir died, to be precise; and lastly the pack of cards.

As you passed jidda and Zahra's room you felt yourself

crumble. You sat down for a moment on their bed, which smelled of lemon—they made scented water from the rinds and used it for the laundry. That smell, mixed with sweat, dirt, and tiredness, was the essence of your daily life, a daily life you considered oppressive but which, now the moment had arrived, you no longer wanted to leave. Why were you leaving? What were you searching for? Giving up seeing your niece grow up, seeing your mother get old, protecting your brother, your little brother. What would become of them?

You had spent years dreaming of this moment, convinced that you would never truly be able to be yourself in Morocco, that everything—the life, the house, the neighborhood, your responsibilities—would never stop clipping your wings. Far from there you would be able to start again from scratch, be whoever you wanted to be. But didn't choosing who you wanted to be mean deciding to be someone else? Did you really need to cross the sea to find yourself? Weren't you already there, was it not you who postponed leaving, who beat Samir at cards, who kissed the palms of jidda's hands?

The choice, in reality, wasn't yours. This thing too, like all the other things, was happening to you. It had already happened. You couldn't stop it. And not because you were special; in fact precisely because you weren't. You weren't leaving for glory, but to look after your family. You wouldn't conquer Europe—you would be an economic migrant like all the others. Like all the others, you would hide in the belly of a ferry for Barcelona. You wouldn't conquer Berlin. You would go to France to work, in the best-case scenario, as a dishwasher in some fancy restaurant; you'd live in a room with ten other Moroccans and a smelly bathroom, sending all your money home and hoping to return in the summer. You were no different.

You left a note for jidda and Zahra.

You were about to leave their room when the door opened slightly and through the crack you saw Idris's eyes. He made you jump but you beckoned him in. He closed the door behind him and leaned against it, eyes staring at the floor.

Are you ready?

No, you coughed, hiding the quake in your voice with a laugh.

Listen—he said with a strangely energetic tone—you have to promise me something.

You looked up. He looked even skinnier now, a pile of bones. How had you not noticed it before? When had he gotten so thin? He turned his stupid Walkman and the photo of your baba over in his hands. His eyes were still lowered. He couldn't stand still and was shifting his weight from one foot to the other.

What?

He swallowed. He waited a minute, then swallowed again.

That as soon as you get yourself sorted you'll come and get me.

You stood up and walked toward him, not knowing what to do. He didn't let you hug him—you were holding yourselves together on too thin a thread. Your hand on his shoulder, his on yours. You had taken him to school. You had scooped him up off the ground. You had dressed him in your clothes, and you had hated him. You had defended him, and you had accused him. He was yours.

There's an old woman I take a bit of shopping to once a week, you said, and you gave him the address of the lady who had hidden you under her mattress. Idris nodded, without asking who she was or why you owed her.

And Boubakar?

Ah! You need to leave a tiny bit of weed on his bedside table, and hide the rest, otherwise he'll smoke it all at once. And you'll do this every day. He'll never ask you where it is.

You both laughed. He put his Walkman into your hand.

Take it, he said, so you won't feel lonely . . .

His hands in yours. Another pause, a very long one. You nodded.

Bsslama, little brother.

Boubakar waited for you downstairs on his bike. Neither of you said a single word.

Part Three

1.

My Mina,

I'm sorry. Please take care of Berta, I know it's difficult, but Aisha can't do it on her own. The bar is everything I've created in my life, apart from the two of you, and I would like you to look after it together. Maybe it will give you a way to remember me.

I held your final instructions in my hand. They were words I wasn't looking for and didn't want. You had betrayed me once again: the last in a long line of evidence that you didn't know me, and you didn't give a damn about what was best for me. Why did you never ask me when you were alive? I stopped reading after the first paragraph and shoved the piece of paper in my pocket.

We don't *have* to do it, said Aisha, looking at me sideways. I didn't think about how much my indignation might be hurting her, how rejected she might be feeling. She had proudly shown me everything she had built. She wanted me to like it. Maybe she hoped I would want to stay.

I didn't do what you wanted, did I, Papà? I followed in your footsteps; I fledged the nest. I made a life for myself. I reinvented myself. Nobody there knew our past and I could easily forget it, like an old jacket in the back of the wardrobe. Being there, if it wasn't happiness, was at least relief. You never looked back, so why should I?

I lit a cigarette, my elbows planted on the counter and my face drained. I looked at her, one eyebrow raised.

He told you about this, right? You already knew.

Aisha shook her head. As if—he never told me anything. I wouldn't have let him do it. I know you hate being here.

She smiled at me, a sad and tender smile, sincere and innocent. Suddenly I saw her the same way I did when we were both under ten and she taught me to tie my shoelaces, and then when we were teenagers and she was already a woman, because she had to be. I saw her with the worries and responsibilities that came with being the bigger sister, which I'd never had. How many things had she protected me from? How many other things had she kept quiet so that I wouldn't have to feel guilty? What did she see in that moment, looking at me—did she still see me as a child? Did she still recognize me, despite my attempted metamorphoses? Where do the versions of ourselves go when we reject them? The obsolete, boring, infantile ones, the ones that weren't interesting or informed enough, the ignorant, the selfish, the true?

I don't hate being here, I said slowly, but I can't just drop my whole life.

No, I'm sure you can't, Aisha sighed, and I don't get why he asked you, honestly. Things haven't been going well for a while now, money is a problem, paying the pizzo is a problem, it's all falling to pieces. I don't see why you should have to crawl back into this black hole when you've built your perfect life over there. You made your choice a long time ago, if he'd wanted to convince you to come back he'd have had more luck doing it alive than dead.

My perfect life, I thought. My solitary walks. The roar of everyone else's laughter and mine less certain, but loud enough to make me seem happy. Money to spend on instant gratification. I checked my account ten, twenty times a day, counting the money, counting the money. I spent hours at night entering online competitions on the websites of magazines like *Cosmopolitan* or *Elle*, which each month gifted a few lucky people perfumes, flowers, books, sometimes a year's supply of tea or chocolate. All I had to do to enter was put in my personal information, information they'd go on using until the day I died to try to sell me those same products I had once hoped to win. I inserted my name and surname, email, and address, my face illuminated by the screen, and felt nothing. Colleagues' promotions celebrated through gritted teeth; a timid photo on my feed to commemorate a weekend spent in the countryside with friendly acquaintances, with whom I'd had tipsy conversations about life, always careful not to veer into the trap of intimacy; getting drunk with whoever, laughing awkwardly. Having lunch alone in sterile places where I ordered avocado on toast which I didn't even like. Walking along the high street and feeling powerful because I could do whatever I wanted—go to the cinema alone, to enjoy the film; spend Saturday alone in bed having danced all of Friday night; vacations alone, finding myself in Vietnam or Iceland. Parents hardly mentioned, just to say that I hadn't seen them for two years, because I was too busy, too far away.

Let's see how it goes, I said, turning the piece of paper over in my hands as I looked distractedly around.

There was a man sitting outside with four other guys. He had thick, dark curly hair which shone where the sun hit it. The others were playing cards, and he was reading a book. I squinted to see the cover. Our eyes met for a second. He smiled with all of his teeth. What courage, I thought, to smile like that, as if he had nothing to hide.

Aisha waved and beckoned him over.

Mina, this is Nazim. Nazim works for Médecins Sans Frontières and gives me a hand with some of my projects.

Nazim smiled in a sad way.

Used to work, he corrected her.

We shook hands. I noticed the way his forehead wrinkled, the curious lingering of his eyes on the tip of my chin and my wrists as I nervously tucked my hair behind my ears, and I felt suddenly caught in a moment of intimacy.

He wasn't very tall, his eyes were green and bright, a little distant, making him look slightly dazed. He moved clumsily, as if he didn't know what to do with his body, because he didn't like it. One day, some time later, he told me that he no longer liked bodies in general, not even women's. He had seen too many floating in agitated waters for long seconds before sinking, watched them descend into the darkness. He didn't like going to the beach, because he couldn't help wondering whether the bodies drying off in the sun were, in another life, the same ones who died submerged like shipwrecks with no treasure. Walking, drinking a beer alone on his balcony, going up and down the supermarket aisles, he still heard the lost voices in the deafening roar of the sea. They scared him and also, in a strange way, gave him comfort.

I'm so sorry about your dad, he said. He was an extraordinary person, we'll miss him more than words can say. Truly.

I fear you knew him better than I did.

Aisha went to put a hand on my shoulder, but resisted the impulse at the last moment and retracted it, as if she'd been burnt.

Why do you say that? He asked, without surprise or judgment.

I shrugged and looked away. It's not really your business, I said dismissively.

True, he replied, unruffled. Sorry, I heard him talk about you so much that I feel like I know you. He turned toward Aisha, looking for confirmation, and she shrugged as if to say: do as you wish, don't let me get in the way. He made a silent decision and sat down next to me.

The first thing you have to know about me is that I can be a bit intrusive, he continued. I like to share. People usually learn to trust me. Ask me whatever you want.

I burst out laughing. That's a bit presumptuous of you.

He shrugged. I am presumptuous.

I felt a strange sense of pride rising in me, it felt important to be clear that I wasn't someone he could get close to. I know your type, I said. The books, the nonchalance, your breezy little smile that screams privilege. The city is full of people like you. They're usually the ones who were born rich, graduated from Oxford with a degree in History of Medieval Music or something, and then inexplicably find work in massive companies thanks to their "creative flexibility."

Nazim didn't seem bothered by my derisive tone. He didn't seem ashamed of anything, least of all his smile. He tilted his head and dramatically massaged his chest, as if I had hit him. His amused gaze grabbed me like a lasso, and I felt I needed to wriggle out of his subtle grip.

Languages, he conceded. At Cambridge.

I nodded, satisfied. Of course.

Nazim is a cultural mediator. He works on the rescue boats and in the reception centers, Aisha intervened, anxiously trying to smooth any tension, as if she were somehow endangered by my natural antipathy for this guy.

So you're educated, rich, and a white savior?

He burst out laughing. Hmm, when you put it like that I sound like a three-headed monster. Luckily at least a couple of them have been decapitated.

Oh, no! What happened?

He took a deep breath. I got stuck in the little wrinkles at the corners of his eyes. He had moles dotted all over his face—I studied them while waiting for his answer, which didn't take long to come.

My father ran a travel agency that won the contract for

Costa Cruises: he was the one who managed the dockings, the activities offered to the tourists, the partnerships with restaurants . . . You're right, I grew up in a rich family. We had a house with a swimming pool, a maid, a company car, things like that. Dad obviously wanted me to continue the family business, so he sent me to study abroad. He would have liked me to do economics, but I didn't have the right kind of brain for it, so languages had to do. I was always an intelligent kid—I raised an eyebrow at that affirmation, and he flashed a cheeky smile that I couldn't help finding attractive—and he had very high hopes for my future.

It sounds like you weren't that involved in the decision, I commented.

Nazim shrugged: I'm an only child, I've never had much choice. And I've never been good at making decisions for myself, I'm too spoilt. After finishing university, I went back to Istanbul to take over the company. It was fun, actually. I was surrounded by people, by things. I never stopped to ask myself whether it was what I wanted—it had to be and that was it.

He paused for a minute. Then Erdogan came into power. There were some attacks. People stopped coming to Turkey. The routes of the cruise ships were changed one after the other. The customers disappeared. It was all over within the course of a year.

I didn't want to feel empathy for him, I wanted to find him unpleasant and opinionated—because he was, as I was. Yet there was something defenseless in the way he spoke. He seemed to not worry in the slightest about whether or not he was interesting to others. He emanated a sense of himself that was different from Liz's threatening confidence, or the obsequious and indifferent ways of the people in the city. He was looking at me and he didn't seem to confuse me with his own reflection. He didn't seem to be playing a game. He wasn't trying to impress me, defeat me, seduce me or overpower me. He was looking at me, and speaking, and that was all.

My father got sick with sadness. He decided to sell the company. I couldn't bear seeing him like that . . . Someone I knew from Cambridge told me he was going on a boat with an NGO and that they needed a cultural mediator who knew languages . . . and so I found myself on another boat.

We looked at one another. He too was running away from something, but he didn't feel the need to hide it.

How's your father now? I asked him, and my voice came out low and soft, as if wanting to dampen the blow of the response. He took a sip of his tea. I had an acute sense that he was putting his ideas in order. Perhaps he had exposed too much of himself, perhaps he had hurt himself.

It's strange, he said after a long pause. He will never tell me what he feels, but I know, I can sense it. I can see that he spends the whole day in his pajamas in front of the TV drinking beer, not seeing anyone, not doing anything. He had to sell the house and now he and my mother are in their old apartment from when they were first married . . . Even if I wanted to go and see them there would be nowhere for me to sleep. I haven't seen them for three years . . . But this place reminds me of them, somehow.

Don't you get bored here?

It was a question that scared me, as if I were sifting through options I didn't really believe I had.

He smiled: sometimes, yes, but living here has its surprises.

For example?

You, for example. His smile widened and made his reddish moustache quiver. You are certainly unexpected.

I was taken aback and didn't know how to respond. I looked away.

He took a handful of coins out of his pocket and left a few of them on the table. The rest he put into a jar with a piece of paper stuck on it that said "Hassan."

Are you staying a few more days? He asked, getting up and

putting on a light, creased jacket. My grandmother would have said it looked like it'd been pulled out of a donkey's ass.

I don't know, I responded, I don't exactly feel at ease here.

He nodded. Maybe being uncomfortable can teach you something.

You know, before you say something you should always repeat it a couple of times in your head, so you know how arrogant it will sound when it comes out.

He laughed, now at the door. What I wanted to say was: stay a while longer. He paused. I want to talk some more.

And with that he left. I found myself watching him through the colored glass of the door, which turned the figure of his back into a kind of broken harlequin.

I heard stifled laughter coming from behind the bar.

Jesus, I said shaking my head, my voice cracking from the irritability. What a know-it-all!

Aisha laughed a bit more. I looked at her, irked: What?

You two are the same.

What? I am *not* that opinionated.

Oh yes you are. You both come and go with this restlessness and then think you've discovered God knows what and that your truth applies to everyone. It's not arrogance, it's just that you are both so desperate for someone to tell you you're right. As if that could somehow save you.

I looked at her sideways: When did you become so wise?

She shot me a cutting look and adjusted her headscarf. Me, wise? No no, I haven't travelled, I've always just lived here, I don't know the world, I can't be informed about real life, can I? I'm just a Muslim, submitting to Allah.

I grabbed a tangerine from a basket on the counter and threw it to her. She caught it and gave me half. There was resentment between us, but not just that.

2.

The weeks passed without me noticing. I was moving around the house as if I had never left. I went back to sleeping naked because of the heat, waking up when the sun seeped through the blinds, sitting in my old place at the table, the one with a view of the sea. I knew where things were: the clothes pegs, the salt and spices, the coffee, the ant traps, the clean bedsheets. I knew which bread to buy and how much it cost, I knew which medicines Nonna had to take, I knew Aisha's timetable at the refugee center and had memorized the phone number of the bar. It only took a few days to pick up from where I left off in this daily life I had worked so hard to forget.

Sometimes I saw you playing cards at the kitchen table, always alone.

Berta was in a state of unconsciousness. She had been for thirty years by this point. But in that period I realized, perhaps for the first time, that her distance from reality wasn't accidental, but a calculated choice. It wasn't your death that made her that way. Berta had been living in a place where we couldn't reach her ever since I could remember.

But she was still my mother, you know? And you were dead, and I wanted to talk about it. I wanted to talk about it to her. I wanted to say to her—and this terrified me, because I suspected she was the only one who understood it—that I was scared nothing you told me was true. I was scared that I actually knew nothing about you. That I'd turned my back on the opportunity to know you, to know where I come from, who I had got certain things that scare me from, if you too at times saw things that weren't there, if you too struggled to breathe. I wanted to search for you in her memories and in my own flaws, so that I could learn to like them. I wanted to build a channel of communication with the past you, to tell you to wait for me, to tell you I'd come back.

I couldn't remember the last time we'd spoken, but your stories kept me awake at night.

One morning, while I smoked on the swing in the garden, in the creaking silence of the iron and the cicadas, I asked Berta what you were really like. I regretted it immediately, because the question shook her and she turned to look at me as if she had been stirred from a long sleep. The contrast with the usual Berta made her firm eyes look even more solemn.

Your father was a good man. Most of the time I thought I didn't deserve him, she said quietly, with her thick, round glasses, silvering hair swayed by the wind, and every slight movement accompanied by the jingling of her bangles. He was a good man, but he was also difficult. He was quiet, solitary. I wanted to tell him more things than I told him in a lifetime, and I wanted him to tell me many more, and truer. But successful marriages are made of long silences.

I'm scared that I didn't really know him.

Berta smiled. Oh, me too, you know. But does it matter? I think he was happy, Mina. We were always very careful to protect one another, to love one another. I made a lot of sacrifices. He wanted a wife, and I was his wife. I liked spoiling him. He was my only concern. We were two frightened children when we met. I wanted security, because . . . well, you know your Nonna. And he wanted a family. He wanted to belong to someone, to something, he wanted children . . .

Hearing her say it was you who wanted us didn't surprise me. It couldn't have been Berta's idea: she neglected us too much. You were her concern. We were nothing but a wish granted.

With a jolt of awareness, she asked me what kind of mother she had been. She spoke in the past tense, as if we had now admitted that, since you were dead, we no longer belonged to her. Maybe we had never truly been hers. Maybe the only thing that united us was your cumbersome, noisy presence.

I told her the truth. That she had been a distracted mother, completely self-absorbed, and sometimes naively nasty. Naivety was not a justification though. In fact, to me it felt like a further affront. Her naivety, the naivety of an eternal child, had forced me to grow up cynical and discouraged. At almost thirty it seemed too late to believe in anything. And yet, as I watched her take in my response, from the corner of my eye, I couldn't help thinking of the time she had taught us how to open our eyes under water, and the funny faces she made, and how much she looked, in moments that now seemed to unfurl in my memory, like the person I would have liked to become. I had always envied her lightness. I looked for it everywhere, outside of me, and I confused it with solitude, with superficiality. I didn't understand that she was not actually light, my mother—on the contrary, she was trapped in a body that had betrayed her, that hadn't been capable of protecting her, that had made her a victim. And so she became unstuck from life, so that she wouldn't have to feel. Observing her now, I almost felt a resigned tenderness toward her: we were so alone, we desired and at the same time feared any kind of intimacy. And this transformed each of our interactions into a miniature battle of misunderstandings. Maybe she wasn't looking at me so that she wouldn't see herself. It felt like we were saying: Is this who you are? And me? I am not this. Or am I?

Since you've been gone, I've understood that the presence

and absence of the two of you in the world will define me and change me day after day. To be the same as or different from you has never been the product of chance, something that just happened to me. Maybe that's why I always felt torn, as if I had been pulled by both arms so hard that my skin ripped down the middle of my chest.

I said nothing about my conversation with Berta to Aisha. Protecting her had become a habit, like everything else. We had slipped swiftly into a timeless, unintentional intimacy. I got undressed in front of her, I showed her the moles I was worried about, the scars, the scratches. When the thoughts in my head became unbearable I woke her in the middle of the night and confessed them like a prayer. She said nothing, just took my hand and waited for me to fall back to sleep between one nightmare and the next. She peed with the door open, her knickers around her ankles, and talked to me. Her hair, under the veil, was turning gray. She showed me. We tested one another, cautiously, awaiting a judgment that never came. Look, look at the hairs under my armpits, my laziness, my fast heartbeat, look at me when I cry for no reason, look at me when I'm incoherent and don't know how to cook. Let me see your extra kilos and your stubbornness, your jealousies, your resentments. Am I still good enough for you? Are we sisters, now?

3.

I intended to bring all of my experience to the bar—cleaning, customer service, targeted marketing. But nothing I had learned in the city worked back home. Putting up little rainbow-colored flags for Pride had no meaning here, and nobody went into raptures over avocado, which people here unceremoniously ate with a spoon. Nobody was interested in food photos on Instagram. The only way to make something work was by word of mouth, and here the word had already gotten around. We were the immigrant bar, period. Making diversity your brand, like everything else, was a fruitful strategy in the city. Here it all seemed mildly ridiculous. Even Aisha couldn't manage to take my safe space sermons seriously.

It's a space where everyone can be themselves, I explained, with a hint of condescension.

But it already is that, said Aisha, a bit irritated by my encroaching on her territory.

Yes, but we have to reclaim it.

Reclaim it from who?

From ourselves! I declared. And from the people of this town.

From where I'm standing it looks like the people of this town think about this way less than you do.

So it's just a coincidence that no one comes near the bar, no one who's white, apart from Nazim and a few people from the university? People speed up when they walk past our sign.

Aisha sighed and looked into the distance, as if the behavior of others was her direct responsibility.

My eyes fell on a photo hanging in a wooden frame behind the bar. It was you and Berta standing in front of the entrance on the day it opened. It was just the two of you but you were smiling, and you looked happy. Didn't you care what other people thought? Were you that strong, that easy-going? The white sign is flaking away now, Papà, and you would no longer be alone, but you're not here.

Do you think it was easier back then? I asked my sister.

Aisha shrugged: Everything was easier in the eighties.

I was about to reply when a stocky man waddled through the door. He was wearing a black polo shirt and outdated sunglasses. I recognized him immediately, though I hadn't seen him in years. He greeted Aisha in an almost camp way and asked her for a coffee. Aisha stiffened and glared at me; I understood that she wanted me to follow her into the kitchen.

Don't say a word, she whispered. Go and make him his coffee.

I went back into the bar and turned on the machine. It'll take a minute—I said in a neutral tone—it needs to heat up.

He nodded without taking off his sunglasses. Never in a hurry, never any money, he said. You're the sister, right? The one who's gone away? My condolences. Nasty business, eh? Nasty business. Your pa was the only negro you could talk to like a Christian. He knew how to play.

I swallowed the insult and the bile. I nodded.

He was different from the others, the guy continued, because he showed respect. Adapting is important.

Aisha came out of the kitchen with an envelope in her hand and passed it to him.

Thanks sweetheart, he said. He sort of grunted when he spoke. Listen, tomorrow we'll kill the pig, I'll bring you a couple of frittole, eh? Capocollo? Go on, it's on the house.

I served him his coffee, which he drank without sugar, arching his long, white neck. Leave the machine on next time, he spat in dialect, this coffee stinks. Explains why this shithole's empty, eh? You don't even know how to make a fucking coffee. And put a sausage sandwich on the menu for fuck's sake, it's the holidays soon.

Aisha said she would add pork to the menu and that we'd keep the coffee machine on in future. She thanked him without looking him in the eye.

He turned to me and, forcing himself to speak Italian, asked: How long you staying?

I don't know yet, I answered.

He nodded, waved goodbye to Aisha, and left without paying for the coffee.

In an effort to attract university students, I set about turning the bar into a co-working space. I stacked old books and vinyls on the shelves to make the vibe more intellectual, modernized the furniture, gave it a hipster touch by ordering an unjustified quantity of accessories from Urban Outfitters. I covered the walls with plants and macramé which cost me an arm and a leg. Liz adored macramé, dream catchers, and all that braided hemp stuff. Naturally so did I.

I like how you're whitewashing the place, Nazim said one day with a smile devoid of indulgence. He was sitting on a pouf in a corner sipping his tea, observing me as I watered the plants and plumped the cushions. I turned to look at him, speechless. In a hot flash of pride I tried to answer back, but all that came out were a handful of convictionless sentences.

First of all, we're closed. What are you doing here? And *you* are accusing *me* of whitewashing? You are so much whiter than me. Do I need to remind you which of us has received an imperialist education, handsomely paid for by his parents?

Nazim shook his head, amused. I'm just saying that if Emma

Watson and Wes Anderson had a teenage daughter who loved Noam Chomsky, this would be her bedroom.

Jesus, you're so pretentious.

Anyway, what do dream catchers have to do with the Maghreb?

Oh, because you're too cool to follow trends, are you? I guess you buy your linen at the market and sew it into clothes yourself, by hand, and I guess you don't have plants in your house, just inherited furniture, stacks of books on the floor and no television, because you're waaay too hip to watch TV. You have subscriptions to the *New Yorker* and *The Atlantic* instead.

He burst out laughing and I glared at him. His presence was setting my nerves on edge. He was so unflappable, so indifferent to all the things that I thought, until a moment before, were important and that, once run under his gaze, appeared superficial and useless. I felt superficial and useless too. How could I be on equal terms with him? He was more educated, richer, more altruistic, more generous—I felt like he could crush me, and I didn't want him to. I didn't want to adapt to his way of thinking, no, I wanted him to know that I wasn't impressed in the slightest. I was looking for a fight. His eyes, so eager and aware when they looked at me, fascinated me, annoyed me, and above all, saw me, me who had made invisibility my thing.

I'm just trying to put my stamp on the place, I said, looking him in the eyes.

All this . . . does it make you feel more at home? He asked, gesturing at the plants and the macramé. My pride immediately collapsed.

I exhaled. No. I stayed silent for a minute, then added: Home is a dangerous word. I risked looking at him and he didn't look confused.

Home as a cage? He suggested.

Home as a glass display cabinet: when I'm inside everyone

observes me from outside. At least in the city nobody looks at me.

My voice cracked. I felt a pain in my chest and a hand instinctively flew up to contain it. Nazim moved closer, a flash of concern in his eyes. Is everything O.K.? He whispered, trying to meet my gaze. I leaned on him for a moment, then pushed him away.

Don't worry. It's been like this since I came back, I keep having these flashes where I feel like my chest is being crushed. Every so often I see him, sitting there. I pointed at the little table with the chessboard on it. I was breathing heavily. And then I see myself as a little girl, my feet dangling from one of the bar stools, and then I see us gargling tea, and think of all the things he told me about his life before, all things I don't know whether they really existed, and suddenly I'm full of doubt about whether I exist either.

There was a short pause; neither of us seemed to know what to say. Nazim held himself at a distance and squared me up hesitantly. Then he seemed to make a decision.

The last mission was tough, he began, strangely without looking at me. They kept us offshore for two weeks waiting for our permits. He ran a hand through his hair and lit a cigarette. It was the first time I'd seen him nervous. You know, the adrenaline of a rescue is like a drug. The danger, the desperation, the fear, the relief, the gratitude. They cling to you for a while—you feel like God, a determiner of whether people live or die. Then there's the boredom. The waiting. I'm not a patient person. I know that I don't do what I do on the boats for other people, I do it for me. A sense of guilt, or of omnipotence, I don't know, but I can't do without it and it's difficult to stare at the empty sea. I become aggressive. One evening . . . the Kurds were fighting over cigarettes because there weren't enough for everyone. The Kurds are always fighting over something, they have war on the brain. And they hate me, because I'm Turkish . . . nobody helped them when they needed it. They provoked me and I was keen. He exhaled a stream of smoke and looked at me, shrugging with a guilty expression on his face. I punched a boy who had arrived here already missing one eye and with his skin covered in scabies. He can't have been more than nineteen, malnourished, dehydrated. A pathetic spectacle: a privileged, educated adult man fighting on the floor with a sack of bones over a couple of cigarettes. I knew when we docked that would be my last mission, at least for a while. And so here I am taking the piss out of you and pretending I don't have any problems.

I put a hand on his shoulder and felt his neck muscle relax under my fingers. Touching him was an easy thing.

He told me how he'd met Aisha at the reception center, a precarious building full of desperate people and good intentions. The regional funds always came late and were never enough. The local people could barely look after themselves, but made a surprising effort to not leave anyone behind; there was something profoundly Christian about saving people at sea—something evangelical that people really believed in. The immigrants weren't treated as equals; they were a charitable project, and that sufficed to mobilize the Christians as much as was needed, in the disorganized and clumsy ways of a population that has never believed in legality, bureaucracy or government help, distant as they have always been from the lazy eye of Rome. For the things you needed, you depended on the criminal organizations, and on God.

Once out of danger, the immigrants were poured back out onto the streets like dirty dishwater, ignored, marginalized, left to die of other deaths. This was the Christian way to save thy neighbor.

A comfortable silence had settled between us. It was nice to be like this with Nazim. I looked around me and for a minute

I thought that there was nothing wrong in that place and that I had no right to change it.

Did my father ever talk to you about the bar in Derb Sultan, the one he and his brothers always went to?

Nazim smiled: Oh, yes! He said it was terrible, like a truck stop. Dirty, plastic chairs and tables . . . nothing like what we imagine when we think of Morocco. He told me . . .

I interrupted him: "Poverty, when you look for it, is the same wherever you go."

Exactly!, he nodded, amused.

What a bastard, I laughed. There was something light in my breath. When I was little and didn't want to eat pasta and beans he would come up close to my face, really serious, and say in an icy tone: "When I was your age I was dying of hunger."

But it's true! It's true that poverty is the same everywhere, if you look for it.

Yes, but why would you look for it?

He picked up a macramé basket and presented it to me with challenge in his eyes. What are these objects? Just a means to show something. But who do you need to show it to, and why? Do you think anyone really cares?

I don't know, I admitted, and immediately plummeted back into my usual labyrinth of obsessions. I had been so busy trying to become a person who could be considered right, but I no longer knew why I did certain things rather than others, I don't know why I sometimes felt like crying when I should have been happy, or why in the middle of a party I often found myself locked in the toilet wondering where the razors are.

You're lost, Nazim roused me, taking one of my hands in his. His touch was warm and light. I felt his rough fingers down to my bones. Everything was amplified. Suddenly I felt surrounded by a crowd of people, observing me, muttering amongst themselves, like in an anatomy class where I was the cadaver. There was a bright light focused on me and their faces were now surprised, now annoyed. They were saying nasty things but I couldn't make them out. I wanted to know what they were saying, and I didn't.

There are too many people, I muttered, burying my face in my hands. I could see them there too.

I was so knotted up that I let myself be guided by his hands, placed firmly on my shoulders. Nazim steered me to the terrace, then down the little steps of the stilt house and onto the beach, where with a gentle push he invited me to sit down on the sand. He took off my shoes and socks, and rubbed the wet sand across the soles of my feet.

Do you feel the grains of sand? What do they feel like?

His hair fell over his face. He didn't look me in the eyes, he didn't invite me to follow him. He just sat there. I closed my eyes.

Wet, I croaked, my voice low and uncertain. Some of them are a bit sharp, they're tickling me.

He made a cup with his hands and splashed my feet with salt water.

It's cold, I said, it's making me feel the wind.

And? What sounds do you hear?

The sound of the waves.

Describe it to me.

It's slow, the sea is calm and dragging the pebbles. It's like a rattle.

And?

And . . . the seagulls. The cicadas. I can smell salt and fish. There's someone cooking with the window open. I can hear voices in the distance, maybe a TV.

I opened my moist eyes and looked at him with half a smile: They're not talking about me.

He shook his head and reciprocated my smile. Then he got up, shaking off the sand, and extended a hand toward me.

4.

I hadn't heard from anyone from my former life since I came back, apart from Liz. As if I had been wiped suddenly away from the city's memory, my shadow had shrunk, illuminated by an eternal midday. I quit by email and received a standard copy-and-pasted reply with my final paycheck attached. My invisible flowing through the folds of the streets, in the noise and the silence, had been translated into an expulsion to which I put up no resistance, and which tasted of abandonment. But I didn't understand who had abandoned who. I felt left behind against my will.

Mostly I missed Liz. I felt her influence evaporating off my sun-burned skin, and it terrified me. I clung on to her image as if, once she disappeared, I too would go, along with everything I thought I had become. I was obsessed with her Instagram. I stared at the photos on her feed: at the theater, a museum, in parks, at the market, summer festivals, in wide open spaces—wide, yes, but not as wide as the sea. I never liked anything and I watched her stories with a fake account. I didn't want her to know how interested I was in her, or the extent to which her life had become the yardstick by which I measured my own.

She looked like she'd lost weight. I screenshotted some of her photos so I could zoom in and compare them with photos from the past. Her body made me hate mine. If she was tagged in a place, I'd go and look for it on Google Maps and imagine myself there with her. But I didn't want to talk to her. I didn't want her to ask me how I was. I didn't want to tell her you were dead, I didn't want her to see me in my grief. We carried on exchanging emptier and emptier, rarer and rarer messages. She had called me a couple of times, but I always had an excuse not to answer, and she very quickly stopped trying. I told myself that what I wanted to hide from her, she didn't want to see. That was how it had always been with us.

But one day, completely out of the blue, she wrote to say that she had rented my room out to someone else. I had taken off without telling her when I was coming back, and I hadn't bothered to keep her in the loop. It wasn't about the money: the rent I paid her was purely symbolic, but maybe someone else needed a place to stay and I wasn't using mine. She was presenting it to me like a gesture of altruism. Hypocrite bitch. I lost my patience, I told her you had died and my mother wasn't eating, hoping she'd be mortified, feel ashamed and embarrassed and drop the subject—but the conversation took an unexpected turn.

I responded to her call at the first ring and heard her howling: I knew it! I knew it! You're a sociopath, Mina, you're fucking crazy!

I had left her alone and I only bothered telling her how good things were, but how could things be so good if my father was dead? She had known something was going on and that I was keeping her out of my life. She seemed angry and wounded. She hadn't realized our closeness was so superficial, but maybe that level of intimacy was the only one we knew.

I'm sorry, I said, capitulating to the game I had contributed to constructing. I'm sorry, I was freaking out. I mean, you get it, right?

She responded with a controlled calmness: We all have our hurt.

My hurt, though, had no restraint: it had consumed everything, even Liz's share. Like when I was at school and my elbow nudged its way over the border constructed by our pencil cases. I had crossed a line. My pain had swollen inside of me and made me cumbersome. I had become selfish; it seemed that nothing of the life we had shared mattered to me anymore. We were friends, but she was on the swing and I was pushing it. Who would push her, now? Was it a question I should have been asking myself?

I said sorry, sorry, sorry until she calmed down. I promised her that from that moment on I would be sincere. The thought of losing her was terrifying. What she said was true: I didn't care about her at all; but I cared about me in relation to her. Liz was the glue that kept all the disparate elements with which I had built myself together. I no longer had much to say about Haim's latest album and what it represented for female empowerment in rock music, or about Annie Ernaux's autofiction, or about the long weekend we were supposed to spend hiking in Norway. I couldn't afford to drift further away.

I dragged myself to the bar in a state of confusion. Mahdi was there and he greeted me with a smile. He seemed happy to see me and I immediately wondered why, what he wanted from me, what I should do to appease him. I was very sad, but I didn't want to hide it or talk about it. So I dug around in his sadness, and he allowed me to with a kindness I didn't deserve.

I asked him if he had been happy since he got here. Was it possible to be happy in a place like this?

It's a calm place, he said.

Calm, I repeated.

Calm heals . . . he sighed and looked at me sideways. But I wish I could go home . . . I dream of it at night. I heard a tremor in his voice, even some resentment. I feel it when I'm grumpy, when I'm sleepy, when I become a child again. All the ugliest things and the most beautiful things about me come from there. I'd walk back there if I could.

He stopped talking and I looked away. Unlike me, he wasn't afraid of his suffering.

I know that I'm lucky, he said quietly. I'm lucky because I'm alive. And perhaps, you know, I'll have a good life here. I'll be safe, I'll have opportunities I would never have had at home; but I'll become a completely different person. I see it already, it's happening now. No, it's already happened. I'm no longer who I was when I left, my body is different, my mind is different. I'll be someone else, and I'll have other things: but I won't get back who I was, what I had.

I nodded, drying my eyes. I looked at the little table with the chessboard that always reminded me of you. He asked me if I ever thought of this place when I was away.

All the time, I responded, I thought about it all the time.

Did you miss it?

I shook my head. It wasn't as much missing, I tried to explain, as an annoying presence that I couldn't free myself of.

I would like to forget my mother the way I last saw her, Mahdi said, his voice low, guilty. So thin, her bones poking out of her clothes, her glassy eyes looking only at memories. I would like to remember her when we were little and she played cops and robbers with us and she would laugh as she chased us around and always let us win. Her eyes shone, she was beautiful, and life was simple. That's how I'd like to think of home. But it wasn't like that when I left.

But you'd go back anyway.

Yes, but it wouldn't make any sense, that house is no longer there.

He wanted to be an architect, he told me, he wanted to go to university. I told him he should go to the north, or to Germany, because there he could realize his dreams, here there was nothing for anyone, and he shouldn't waste all he had given up by staying on that beach that stood sentinel over the dead.

He responded that he didn't care about succeeding; that in truth he just wanted a quiet life, a few friends, a place to build something small and sweet that he could call the present. Now even studying felt like a privilege: he could go to classes because Aisha had changed his shifts to allow him to work and support himself. If he didn't manage to become an architect he would continue working there at the bar, where the memory of his mother was like the memory of so many others, where he didn't feel obliged to honor, or even lay claim to, the death the fear the uncertainty of his brothers. He told me that his greatest joy was the idea of studying for the pleasure of studying. A revolutionary idea, in some ways. He told me that life, all of it, felt like a great gift. He told me that he couldn't wait to be bored; he had experienced a lifetime of emotions and he liked the idea of a quiet happiness.

You know those moments that are sad and really beautiful? He said. Like when you see two old people holding hands as they walk. Or when you meet a person who you haven't seen for a long time, who's no longer part of your life, but when you see each other, you stop and talk and you're happy to have met them, as if nothing had changed. Or when a smell reminds you of something from when you were little and you can't quite identify what it is, but you feel the nostalgia? These are the things I want to experience. Time passing. Time passing is a gift from Allah.

People came in. Mahdi gave me a look of sympathy, maybe compassion, and walked away. Out of the two of us, I was the lost one, the one without an anchor. He, perhaps, had two homelands—however imperfect, unreachable, hard-earned, given up. I had none.

I couldn't stop thinking about Liz.

One time she spent an entire afternoon buzzing ostentatiously around the hob. I sat at the kitchen table and helped her with the little that she allowed me to. But I couldn't move away either: I had to be witness to the efforts she was making for me. She put the food on the table with extreme care, using special bowls she had bought for the occasion. Her taste was impeccable; she often posted photos on her grid of ceramics, cups, mugs, a centerpiece, chopping boards, glasses, vases, full of fruit, vegetables, fresh flowers bought at the organic farmer's market. What is beautiful is also good, and she wanted to be good.

She had written on a piece of white paper, in the handwriting of a dutiful schoolgirl, the Kurdish-Palestinian fusion menu that she was going to serve, with added detail about the origins of the dishes and their political value. When she served up, she put double the amount in my bowl than she put in her own, then spent ten minutes photographing it all from various angles. She posted the photos on her feed with an extremely long caption about the power of food to unite people and about what this could mean for the families forced to leave their homes due to the conflict in the Middle East. Very profound thoughts. I managed to think only of my stomach.

Finally she sat down, rested her elbows on the table with her face between her delicate fists, and stared at me. Go on, eat! She incited.

I said: You eat too. But she had tasted lots while cooking and wasn't hungry anymore.

I stuck a forkful of mansaf in my mouth, forcing myself to chew slowly. I was a bit intimidated, but also very grateful, because she was my friend and she had cooked for me, dedicated time to me. I didn't ask myself what she got in exchange. She carried on watching me as I ate. I was fearful of her judgement, and I tried to glean from her face the appropriate time to stop.

Do you want more? She asked.

What did she think of me? She thought I was a fatty, for sure. A foolish, naïve, provincial, awkward, greedy, insignificant fatty. In the way she looked at me I saw all my flaws and felt ashamed. What I didn't understand, though, was that, in asking me if I wanted to eat more, Liz wasn't thinking about me: she was concentrating on herself, on the dishes she had cooked, on how they would appear to the eyes of her followers, on how *she* would appear. Maybe she wanted my approval, or maybe she wanted to learn how to be a family. Maybe she wanted to tell me that she too felt lonely, sometimes, but I was too focused on myself to see it. We were both egocentric in our own ways. She thought about how to present herself—generous, capable, creative, maternal, caring, a friend, interesting, multicultural, educated, cultured, brilliant. I thought about how she saw me, which was how I would then see myself.

I felt a hand on my neck. I thought: there you are, you've come to find me. But it wasn't you.

Nazim sat down next to me. Wanna play? He had a pack of Spanish cards in his hand. I nodded gratefully. We sat down opposite one another and started our game.

How's it going today?

He looked at me as he asked with those eyes that were always amused. He was wearing a white linen shirt with a mandarin collar, through which I could see a thick mesh of hair. For a moment I imagined running a hand through it, burying my face in his early morning smell, still half asleep.

He rested his face on one hand, like a child cradling himself. He was so gentle to himself; I wondered if he treated everyone he spoke to like that. I wondered if he would hold my face in his hands with the same tenderness.

Shit, I responded sincerely. Once again I felt his gaze opening me like a clam and I didn't understand what was happening; I no longer felt capable of lying, of protecting myself by concealment. I told him everything—about Liz, about our friendship, about how I thought I was in the city, about how I felt about being here, and of how much it disconcerted me, about how different it was from what I remembered, about my resentments.

I even told him that I didn't understand why I always ended up answering his questions. The last bit made him smile.

Am I crazy if I don't know who I am? I asked, hiding behind the cards.

Nazim shook his head and pulled out a card that he should have kept. He didn't have a game plan, he evidently wasn't interested in winning.

Do you miss him, your father?

I shrugged and sniffed and said no.

It was normal for me not to see you, not to hear from you, not to think of you. In my daily life you were nothing but a misleading reflection.

But knowing that I wouldn't see you again, that it was over, for us. That I would no longer be able to tell you I was scared, or ask if you were proud of me. That I would never again smile at you in search of a fleeting hug, or a quick kiss on the forehead as you ruffled my hair, that I wouldn't feel your hand on my neck accompanying me.

Sometimes I used to think: sooner or later we will find each other again and I'll forgive him and it will get better. I'll forgive him for letting Berta hurt us so badly. I'll forgive him for his indifference, or cowardice. I'll forgive him and then we'll be happy, perhaps. I'll go and find him when he's old and I'll tease him for his clumsy movements, and we will be peaceful, free of resentment. I'll also forgive Berta, I'll forgive everyone. Then it'll be easier to come back. One day, when I'm ready.

And your father? I asked Nazim. Do you miss him?

I call him once a week. I talk to my mom on the phone, but I know he's there listening. And when my mom asks me if I'm well, if I have enough money, if there's anything I need, I know it's him asking, really.

How do you know?

Because my mother knows full well that it's me who sends money to them, now. My father has always managed the business, but it's she who gets her hands dirty with the money. When they used to earn a lot, she invested it, now they earn little, she ekes it out, and she has no qualms about getting it where she can—she sells jewelry, property, anything. She has always been a very practical woman. Strong. My father, on the other hand, was born into a modest family that aimed to get rich. For him, obsessed with what other people think, image is everything.

Is that why, I asked, he sent you to study in England? For status?

Yes. He had this romantic idea of Europe, you know, its history, its art. He wanted to belong to them. But we'll never belong to them—not deep down.

Didn't you enjoy Cambridge?

I was the Muslim poster boy of my year—and I'm an atheist, but try explaining that to them. Turks are all Muslims to them, all misogynists, homophobes, hardened smokers, storytellers, swindlers. Me and a dozen others were the diversity quota and we were waved around like fish at the market, everyone wanted to be seen talking to us to show how progressive they were, and everyone addressed me with blatant condescension, without wanting to actually know me. I have never felt so alone in my life. I couldn't wait to go home . . . But at least I seized the opportunity to study my own culture, something I had always neglected. It was nice, while it lasted.

He looked at me with a confused expression and ran a hand through his hair, messing it up even more. What is it? He asked nervously. Why are you looking at me like that?

I'm not looking at you like anything, I lied, taking a sip of my tea.

Nazim lived in his memories and inhabited his present with the same sense of himself, which I had initially thought was arrogant but was actually a resolute kind of lightness, perhaps the kind I had chased my whole life.

It's just that you seem so . . . I don't know. Carefree. I don't know how you do it.

He burst out laughing. Carefree! You think I do this work out of altruism, don't you? He came closer and lowered his voice: Do you know what I like about being a white savior? White saviors don't have to worry about anything: they are so heroic, so outside of normal life that there's no need to function like a normal human, right? And I'm not talking about doing the laundry, washing the dishes, eating at regular times, looking after yourself and the general decorum of life. I'm talking about having a home, friends, a relationship. I'm unable to think about or feel anything. I'm unable to make plans, to make a single decision. I'm paralyzed.

His expression was both proud and irritated at once. Without thinking I laid a hand over his. He took it and brought it to his cheek. His stubbly beard pricked my skin. I came closer. He smelled of the sea.

Ah, I almost forgot, he mumbled. He rummaged in his pockets and gave me a paper bag. It was full of toasted almonds. It emitted a penetrating smell, woody and sweet. I put one in my mouth. It was different from the ones I was used to eating in the city, which tasted of salt or sugar. It monopolized my senses for a few seconds. It was like putting my head underwater. I ran it over my teeth, under my tongue. I sucked it, then bit into it.

I went to lend a hand in Lampedusa and I was thinking of you, he said as he got up. I wanted to bring you something that would sweeten your enforced stay. He pronounced the penultimate word with just a hint of irony.

You were thinking of me? I asked, surprised. He looked away and cleared his throat.

Do you know what would make you feel better?

What?

His mouth cracked into a large smile: Meeting me here tomorrow at four. And he disappeared before I could ask anything else. His apparitions were always so brief, as if he could only stand a few minutes of intimacy at a time.

* * *

I returned home eating the almonds one at a time, slowly. I stopped to look down a little alleyway squeezed between two houses, which looked straight out onto the sea. I could hear the gurgling of the water that tunneled under the stones. When we were little you used to tell us that the gurgling was the stomach of the sea as it digested fish and people. That was why I never managed to swim all the way out to the buoy. The cats were splayed out in a precarious wedge of shadow. I felt the heat of the asphalt under my feet. I felt.

At home, I found Nonna playing rummy with Magda in the garden. They were dressed the same, in shirt dresses with mid-length sleeves bought at the market, four for the price of three. Their bodies sailed in them, placid and soft.

I miss your father, my Nonna said winking at me. He played properly.

I sat down next to her and took her hands in mine. I studied her thick veins and knotty knuckles, her wrinkles and scars. Then I rested my cheek on her palm and closed my eyes. She smelled of soap.

The women in my family had all survived one or more wars, and wore the wounds. As a girl, my Nonna had seen the Nazis shooting people with their hands and foreheads pressed to the wall, not even glimpsing the sky before dying. She had been so scared she peed herself, and not just once. She had seen her present dizzyingly rise and fall. She hadn't believed in tomorrow. As an adult, when I understood what she had done in her twenties, I never asked her if she had killed, and how it had felt to sleep with a pistol. She scared me, but we had a relationship of secret tenderness. She was a woman of few words. She had raised her only child with a cruel, stoic coldness, no sentimentalism. She bought *L'Unità* every day, and *Il Manifesto*. She always ate to keep herself in good health rather than for pleasure. I don't know if she ever loved a man, I don't know if she ever loved anyone. She certainly wasn't a mother to Berta, but I couldn't muster any resentment toward her, even if I vaguely perceived that this, really, was the origin of all my pain. But how could she love after the death she had seen everywhere?

She wasn't sweet, not even when Berta spent the whole day sleeping. Sometimes, though, when we were hungry and Berta told us there was ice cream in the freezer, she would get up in silence and make us eggplant fritters, the only thing she knew how to cook. When we had a toothache it was Nonna who took us to the dentist. However, when Berta once forgot the drop-off time of my school trip, we arrived late and missed the train, and I cried for the whole following week, she told me to quit whining. That was how she was, my Nonna: she thought only of survival. She taught me to mend my clothes, to make a makeshift rucksack, to put up a tent, to smash pine cones with a rock to get to the kernels, to bandage up an arm or a leg, to put on a condom, to read cards, to believe in fortune and laugh in the face of God, to be disgusted by wealth, to be suspicious of people who aren't scared. When I became a woman and Berta pointed and giggled at my blood-stained pants, Nonna made me sit in front of the mirror with my legs wide open and showed me how to study myself, to know myself better. She told me that we women don't need any help to frighten ourselves, but that blackness, that dark blackness that I had between my legs was mine, and it was my job to know exactly what was there and who I was and who I would become. I had to know that I would survive time and losses. It wasn't enough to look at yourself only once. I needed to do it often. She told me that she looked in her mouth too, in search of herself. We are hiding wherever it is dark.

She liked reading out loud. In the mornings she taught Magda Italian, reading and reading and reading, and patiently explaining the meaning of every word. She wasn't maternal, she wasn't caring, but she was generous in the giving of her time—she knew she had so little left—and she was especially so with those who demanded absolutely nothing of her.

When I told her I was leaving she wasn't surprised. She gave me her copy of *The Little Virtues* by Natalia Ginzburg; she said that the English are a population of unimaginative administrators, not to let myself be dragged into their capitalist folly, into the lie of meritocracy—and that I should be careful with my soul, keep it always close.

Your great-grandfather was a farmer and the son of farmers, she told me, and he was the best person I have ever met. He had never read a book: I read them to him, and he didn't understand it all, but he understood what was important. Don't ever think that the essential is something that's only accessible to some. Do not believe anyone who tells you ambition is the desire to join the elites. Become who you are, Mina, that's the only ambition there is.

Then she gave me a Chanel lipstick and some money, telling me to use it to buy flowers and put them on Karl Marx's tomb in Highgate Cemetery. I spent it on beer, keeping the lipstick for myself and never thought of her advice again.

I had a sudden urge to confess in that moment and she cracked up in sonorous laughter. She told me she'd spent her life believing in the class struggle, but that she secretly liked nice things, and in particular those extremely expensive lipsticks, which were in no way better than the normal ones, but they knew how to deceive you. She was ashamed of that innocent vanity. She had thought that sacrificing her favorite lipstick to the memory of Marx might redress her contradictions.

But instead that lipstick served the function of getting you kissed by some limp-dick. She put a hand on my head but held it firm; her touch wasn't a caress. You know, little one, I'm happy you came back. You were searching for yourself too far from home.

I glanced at her cards. The Jack's a duplicate, Nonna.

She shook her head and brought a finger to her lips: Shh, Magda hasn't realized . . .

Then she turned, her eyes glinting: Did you find yourself?

I shrugged: I saw a glimpse, now and then.

We remained in silence for a while, then I asked: Do you think Papà regretted leaving home?

Nonna looked at me, astonished: Why are you asking me something like that?

I shrugged, staring at the tangerine tree you planted when I was born. It seemed to have survived better than me.

Sometimes I think it's impossible to avoid wondering what would have happened if we'd stayed. And that terrifies me.

Nonna thought about it for a few seconds, and when she spoke her voice was firm. I played cards with that man every evening for thirty years and do you know what I came to understand about him? It wasn't a place that made him the man he was. He carried his house on his back, like a snail. As for you . . . Ah, Mina. Have you looked properly in your mouth?

I laughed, embarrassed, and couldn't respond.

She looked at me, serious: What do you feel when you look in the mirror?

The laughter died in my throat. I couldn't tell her that when I looked in the mirror I felt dirty, avoided my own gaze, felt invisible and at the same time bulky, in the way. I told her that when I looked at myself I felt nothing in particular, like every other woman who had been taught to love, but never herself.

Her eyebrows were white and thin. When she frowned they disappeared like two seagull wings under her fifties bangs, the same ones she had always had, because she belonged to a time in which a woman chose a haircut, one that suited the shape of her face, and kept it for life, always going to the same hairdresser, to whom she would never have to explain how she wanted it because it was always done the same.

You haven't found yourself yet, she commented, without judgement. She pressed a finger on my heart, tapping it sweetly: you're in there, not out here.

That was when Magda joined the conversation.

My house, she said, bombs. All gone. She made a wide gesture with her hands, miming the explosion that had razed her neighborhood to the ground. Then in Germany, she went on, the Russians, the hunger. The hunger. Do you know the hunger?

Nonna nodded, her eyes moistened, and put a hand on Magda's arm, revealing an intimacy I'd never seen her have with anyone.

There was nothing, nothing, Magda murmured, bringing a cigarette to her thin lips, which she lit with a match. She puffed out a stream of smoke, then pushed it away with a hand, as if shooing away the memories. No work, no food. Cold. Nothing. After, back to Poland. Nothing. She shook her head. My family is there. My son, my husband. I send the money. The first time, I didn't go back for three years. Three years without my son. Worse than the hunger, worse than the cold.

She was paid to look after Nonna, because we—me, Aisha, and Berta—had to be free to work and live, or do nothing at all.

Magda's son was called Viktor, because having him was a victory and a sacrifice. He had long, blond hair, which he tied at the nape of his neck with a purple hairband he had found on the school playground and slipped into his pocket. Nonna had explained to me that Viktor hated his mother because she wasn't there, and hated his father because he was. He wanted the opposite, but in reality he didn't know if his life would have been happier. He was in love with the boy who sat next to him in class, and for this he punished himself with the worst of all evils: solitude. He didn't have any friends. He hated Poland and its grayness, he wanted to wear skin-tight jeans and dance, dance like Elio in that film set in Italy that he had secretly downloaded, that he watched and rewatched whenever his father was out. He would watch the scene with the peach and go wild with pleasure and desire. When they were at home together, father and son, they sat in front of the TV, each with their own tray, and ate in silence, both pretending to be alone. They didn't have a sofa, they sat on two old armchairs. His father worked all day and then went out to drink. Maybe, if they moved to a bigger city like Warsaw, Viktor might find a place where he could exist undisturbed. Someone to talk to. Maybe, one day, he would leave, achieving his dream of joining Magda in Italy.

Berta told me, in her rarefied voice, that Magda was very happy with us, that she and Nonna had a special relationship. She said it without any resentment about the fact that she, with her mother, did not have a special relationship. After all, they were free women and relationships tend to bind you, trap you, make you vulnerable, make you a victim, make you an executioner. The lucky ones among us are frightened of cages—the others, of hunger.

5.

The next day, on Nazim's request, I went to the bar at four. When I'd asked Aisha if she knew anything, she had chuckled with a glint in her eye. Tomorrow will be a good day, she had said.

Not knowing what to expect, I felt a strange sense of anxiety as I walked to the door. The idea that there might be some happy or joyous occasion I'd be expected to enthusiastically take part in made me feel like I was being tested: what if I wasn't sufficiently happy? Sufficiently smiley, pleasant, generous, genuine? After weeks spent rubbing up against a reality I thought I hated, I seemed to have discovered that I was no longer capable of pretending. Yet the prospect of accepting whatever mood I was in at any given moment and showing it to others, just as it was, felt like a luxury I couldn't afford.

I walked in. There were many people, more than usual, but each of them was pretending not to know why they were gathered there—as if it was pure chance. There was an electricity in the air, a sense of anticipation. I scanned the bar for Nazim. He winked at me. I felt my shoulders relax under his kind gaze; the chair felt more comfortable, and I stopped feeling out of place.

Suddenly Aisha came out of the kitchen with a cake. It was a normal cake, lemon, bought at the bakery in town. I figured out that it was Hassan's birthday, a boy of just twenty who pottered around working as a bricklayer and spoke Italian very slowly, with a quiet, childish voice and a vaguely French accent.

Hassan smiled as everybody sang happy birthday in a mixture of languages and melodies, clapping their hands, hugging him and laughing. Aisha had left her dugout behind the bar and, surrounded by people, cut the cake and distributed spoons, playing mother hen with joy and tenderness. I found myself behind the bar again in her place. I collected glasses, lit the gas for tea. It was nice to witness that scene and I wanted to contribute, to feel part of it. I brought a bunch of mint to my nose and its intense perfume immediately made me aware of my roots, my mycelium: I was concealed, invisible, but connected to the ground by thousands of tiny threads, a network of memories.

I intuitively knew where the cane sugar was, the ground black tea and the teapot, so encrusted and blackened it gave the drink a flavor a kettle could never recreate. I poured the tea into the cups and back into the teapot over and over again. I did it to make myself useful and therefore visible to the others, but not to be accepted: I was already part. Those people weren't mine, but they weren't other to me either.

Nazim, sitting on a bar stool, passed a finger across my top lip to collect a few drops of sweat. I caught it between my teeth and bit gently. What we were to one another we didn't know, but when he touched me in that way, so unexpectedly, innocent and intimate, I felt as if his hand had already been over my whole body.

I saw him give Aisha a look, and her nod back. Then he leaned forward and whispered in my ear to follow him. He took the jar that was on the counter. It was empty, apart from a rolled-up sheet of paper.

We moved over to the group, which opened up to welcome us in. Then Nazim said to Hassan, in French, that they had got him a present. He passed him the jar. Hassan looked confused, but when he pulled out the piece of paper and read it, he burst into tears, laughing and shouting, hugging everyone there, kissing them three, four times on each cheek. He stamped his feet, clapped his hands, thanked Allah.

We've been collecting the money for six months, Nazim explained to me. All the customers have contributed. Well, some thought it was a tip jar . . . no harm done.

What is it?

A plane ticket—to go home. Nazim squeezed my hand. His eyes were wet, half closed in a sweet smile. I caught a glimpse of Mahdi crying for joy among the others. Maybe he was thinking of his mother. Then I looked at Aisha watching everyone—her eyes were bright but her lips were tight, as if immersed in the happiness of the moment but feeling guilty at the same time. I could tell that she was thinking of you. I knew that every moment of happiness was a moment in which, for a second, she had forgotten you. I wondered if a hand ever reached her from the other side of her walls, if she was ever touched in the dark, with desire, tenderness.

I went over to her in silence and rested my chin on her shoulder. She started, like she always did when I touched her.

Aisha, do you have someone?

She didn't turn to look at me, her expression didn't change. I did notice, though, that her jaw tightened almost imperceptibly, the veins on her neck became a little more visible, her shoulder slightly harder, more tense.

I don't like men, she said, in a neutral tone.

It was the first time she had admitted it to me.

I know, I said, and forced myself to conceal the excitement I felt to have finally deserved that whispered confession, the secret that separated her from others but not from me, not anymore: I was with her, now.

I didn't say "a man," I clarified, I said someone.

She always touched her hijab when she was about to lose control, followed its edge across her forehead with her long, thin fingers, like the old ladies in town with their rosary beads.

You know?

I smiled, lightly shaking my head, surrendering to her vulnerability, her invincible strength. I put my arm around her shoulders and squeezed her. She, for once, didn't move away. We remained for a while like that, as the bar resounded with a festive din. My feet felt heavy.

6.

An integral part of the allure of the city was the way she made me feel, as if it were a conscious action on her part, which I experienced passively. The city was a woman with flame-red lipstick, like the buses and old phone boxes. She was intriguing and seductive. She smoked, and the smoke she spewed from her lips was the early morning fog; it was the pale light of streetlamps at night when I came home in just enough of a stupor that I merged with the asphalt, that a foreign language felt familiar.

The town didn't have, to my eyes, the face of a woman. It was an expanse of houses and sea, and that was all. When I ran from one side of town to the other it didn't speak to me, didn't shape me, didn't complete me. I couldn't escape myself. But I was living there, and my presence was noted. The English girl, they called me—condemning me to foreignness in every place. They were always twitchy in my presence, because I was the daughter of Berta the strange, and the one who had gone to live abroad, and God knows what she has seen and learnt. She looks down at us, the bitch. Who does she think she is? She grew up on the same murky water as the rest of us, only hers was dirtier, the Italafricana. This is what they thought; this is what they whispered in the newsagents or when walking along the seafront. To tell the truth, no one spoke to me at all if not with a kind of deference mixed with suspicion. The same suspicion they probably saw in my eyes. Yet I tortured myself with their judgments so that I wouldn't have to think of you and how your features were starting to blur. Your elongated face, your pointed chin, your aquiline nose. I wondered if that was how they really were. Was I misremembering? Your front teeth, am I mistaken in seeing them overlapping a bit? You hated going to the dentist, to any doctor actually. The concept of getting hurt and then getting healed was somehow foreign to you: life hurts sometimes. Why try to change it?

I found myself putting your shoes on at night. My feet swam in them, despite having put three insoles in. I wanted to run in those shoes, but I was stumbling over my own feet—maybe I was doing it on purpose, to hear you laughing in my head. When that stopped working and I felt like an orphan, I went and picked a fight with Berta like a teenager. I wanted her to notice me, to tell me I was fat and hairy and ugly and stupid. But she was less and less there.

I used to think that not having a mother at all would be better than having her, but now that I saw her disappearing—hidden under a sheet, getting thinner and thinner, her eyes absent—the prospect of losing her terrified me. I hated her but I couldn't live without her, and neither of the two things was in any way avoidable. She didn't get out of bed for days, maybe to avoid having to notice your absence.

Weeks passed and still nothing was done with your ashes, because we couldn't talk about them in the house and she didn't want to see them. We kept them hidden in a jar under our bed. You were hunkering down there, and every night I woke up and checked you hadn't gone anywhere, hadn't left me for the last time. Just naming you in front of her made Berta explode with a violence I'd never seen before. She broke chairs and glasses and screamed at us that we were shits, useless creatures she wished she'd never given birth to. Nothing new, really, but what worried us was the weakness of her voice, how she tired more easily day by day, in a hunger strike that was the slowest death of all. Part of me wanted her to get stronger because if she didn't she'd never be able to say sorry to me, and then we would never be able to make up and I would be a true orphan forever, not because you were both dead, but because you had both died without me knowing whether or not I was loved.

I observed the patience with which Aisha took care of her: how she cooked her porridge with goji berries in the mornings—sometimes she even made a game out of feeding her, pretending it was normal; how she convinced her to get up, to do a bit of stretching; how she rolled her weed, the care with which she mixed it together with orange-scented tobacco. Berta never thanked her. A life spent in the trenches of friendly fire, a choice made to protect herself, a choice as painful and as dignified as my choice to run away and free myself, and to remember, and to cultivate in my stomach a garden of poison. Or not.

I too found myself trapped in the inevitable, primal urge to look after. I decided to buy some peaches one day because Berta loved them and I hoped they would pull her out of bed and make her take on some sugar. I tried not to think too much about why it was so crucial, for me, that she started to resemble the perpetrator again, rather than the victim.

Aisha had warned me not to go to the grocer at the end of the road, because he was an oaf. So I ventured into the alleyways of the town, my eyes lowered and my shoulders rigid. I didn't need to think about where to go, or to check the directions or opening times or reviews on my phone. I knew every single shop, who owned it, who worked there, who their relatives were. Yet, in that topographical memory, in that familiarity, in the way in which my body moved decisively, present and active in the space, I felt uneasy. I hoped nobody would recognize or stop me.

At the shop I chatted with the grocer's daughter, who was a grade or two below me in school and now her belly was swollen like a watermelon and her face aglow with the contentment of someone who is carrying out her role in the world. I felt a surprising sense of understanding toward her. I couldn't stand people who had children because of boredom or naivety, or because of love, vanity, or error. But having a child simply because of life, with a resigned serenity, because our bodies know how—that I could understand. Not like a decision, but like a thing that happens; not a mistake, but an accident. Having children because of nature, I suppose. Like the animals that we are.

It's a little girl, she said stroking her stomach, her cheeks rosy. She was happy, and this moved me almost to tears. We weren't close, but my reaction didn't seem to unsettle her in the slightest. Naturally she knew you had died, and she knew that I never came home and that my mother didn't eat and all the other things that get whispered in the line for the doctor's or the Post Office.

How are things at home? She asked. I told her I was trying to make my mother eat and she gave me her best peaches, picked out by hand, and didn't let me pay.

I'm happy you're back, she smiled, putting the paper bag in my arms with a determined kindness. Everyone's leaving these days. Sometimes entire days go by and I've only chatted to old people. Come and see me some time, we'll have a coffee.

She left her proposal suspended mid-air, not expecting a response. It was just a thing people said, but I knew that if I really did turn up at her house one day she wouldn't be surprised, and it would make her happy.

One day when Aisha was out I found myself counting the minutes that Berta was in the bathroom, my heart in my throat waiting for her to come out, slowly but in one piece. The relief of the door squeaking open wasn't coming. I told myself it was nothing—who knew when she'd last taken a shit? But I couldn't think about anything else.

I moved closer to the door, my ear pushing against the light wood, my fingers on the handle. I heard the water running. I was scared that she had fainted or dozed off in the bath and so, without warning, I opened the door and shouted: Mamma! In my mind, suddenly crystal clear, was my need for her.

She was awake. In the wide tub her body looked like that of a child. She was crying.

My hair fell out, she said, extending a blonde clump in my direction. Just like that, when I was shampooing . . . is there a hole in my head?

I moved closer and took the tangle of hair from her hand. It was a lot. I checked her head. It was more scarce in some areas, but she didn't have any real holes. It's all O.K., I told her, don't worry. If you start eating a bit again it'll grow back.

She stayed silent, her tears falling into the still water, her chin resting on her knees.

I'm ashamed, she said, I'm dirty since he's gone.

Dirty? I asked, surprised.

She nodded. He bathed me, she mumbled as if she were revealing a secret. He scrubbed my back with the glove. He washed my hair like in *Out of Africa*.

I wasn't sure how to respond. I knelt down at the end of the bathtub and let my hands move instinctively, reattuning to the secret language that links a daughter to her mother. I took the soap and the glove and started to delicately rub her skin. I saw her relax, she lifted her arms up without me asking, bent and turned in silence, her body speaking to mine. Then she lay down, curved her head back and let me rinse her hair. Clusters of her fine hair remained in my hand. I didn't say anything.

Mina, she said suddenly, almost distractedly, can I be "mamma" again?

I thought: Here we are, now you can't be wife you want to be mamma again. Now I have a function. I did all I could to ignore the fact that my body was burning with a ferocious joy at the idea that she might need me, that she might be able to see me.

I don't know, I responded with a crack in my voice, let's see.

7.

I was running along the seafront at sunset. It was the only time of day when I felt I would never lose you. It was an intimate space, inside my body, where I was convinced that you were alive. And thanks to which I managed to feel my flesh, which I had so hated my whole life, as something lovable, strong, resilient.

The sea calmed me. I stopped to watch the red ball dip below the line of the horizon. All of a sudden I saw Nazim sitting on the beach. He was smoking and reading the newspaper next to a pair of old men with fishing rods. I went over and sat down next to him without speaking. I liked meeting him by chance every time. I liked that we hadn't exchanged phone numbers and that, even without looking for one another, we met almost every day.

He smiled at me as if I had just appeared on his doorstep.

Hi, he said.

Hi, I said.

We looked at one another in silence and I felt a slight tension, almost an expectation, worming its way into the comfort I always felt in his presence.

What does the paper say?

Oh, the usual things. The world is ending, we're all going to die.

He also seemed uneasy. I asked him if he was well. He shrugged and turned toward the sea, avoiding my gaze, maybe for the first time since I'd met him.

I can't handle myself when I'm alone for too long, he said. If Tangerinn had slot machines I'd be a gambling addict by now.

I replied that I was an expert in solitude and I could offer him private lessons if he wanted.

How can that be, with your *oh so interesting* life?

Oh fuck off, I muttered.

He burst out laughing, a liberatory laugh that lasted longer than it should have. Sorry, he chuckled, I'm not laughing at you.

It's O.K.. I'm happy my ridiculous life brings you joy.

Nazim furrowed his eyebrows, suddenly alarmed, and put a hand on my arm: I don't think your life is ridiculous.

Yes you do. But I can't blame you—it probably is a bit. I don't know, sometimes I feel like I'm trying to do a puzzle, but the image doesn't correspond to the pieces on the table.

Perhaps you don't need to worry about creating the whole picture, he suggested, but rather concentrate on the individual pieces. What I mean is: what do you really like doing? That's who you are, in the end, isn't it? What do you eat when you're alone in the house? What music do you listen to when you run? What do you like to do? *What do you want*?

I let out a stream of smoke.

He laughed through his nose: O.K., yes, nice response. But it's true.

I thought about it a bit. His questions made me curious. He made me curious. He was lying with his legs crossed, his torso raised, propped up on his elbows, his head lolling forward, his eyes half-closed. I had obviously never looked at him properly before, because that was the first time I noticed the freckles around his nose. I felt like laughing, but I wasn't sure why.

What do you like? I asked.

He opened one eye to scrutinize me for a moment, amused. I like poems, he said. Hikmet, Antonella Anedda, Gregory Corso, and Robert Frost. I like orecchiette with pesto. I like rap music. And when you're smoking weed with lots of people and as soon as someone laughs everyone laughs and no one can stop. I like kebabs, but the ones from home, with ground meat cooked on skewers, not the ones they make here. I like dates, and drinking milk directly from the carton. I like it when I'm on a boat and I feel the wind on my face. I like introducing myself to people and watching them say their name. I like walking around the town and observing other people's lives through their open windows. I like the old people in this place. They remind me of home. I like the slowness, and . . . I like talking to you. Then, he said slowly: I like your neck. Now it's your turn, he said, looking at me sideways.

I clicked the roof of my mouth with my tongue, opened it to formulate an answer, even at the cost of making one up, but I just couldn't. Nothing came to mind. I don't know how to play this game, I said. All of a sudden I felt so lost I wanted to cry.

Hey, hey. He put his hands around my face, drumming his fingers lightly on my temples. He rested his forehead on mine. Don't worry. I didn't mean to stress you out.

I feel pathetic, I gasped.

You are not pathetic, it takes guts to go around telling everyone: look at me, I'm broken here and here and here! And I for one feel less alone every time I see you.

His lips stopped a breath away from mine. Almost brushing them, a caress. He was asking my permission. A sigh escaped from my mouth. When he finally put his mouth over mine, he opened my lips determinedly, his hands slipped into my hair, I felt the pressure of his body against me and I was immediately used to that comforting, warm contact, inexplicably natural like a habit I didn't know I had. It felt strange to pull apart.

I scrutinized his darkened expression: What's up? Did I bite you?

He smiled, shaking his head. I'm the pathetic one, he started explaining, I'm unreliable. I have never truly finished anything. I dodge life, I don't want responsibilities . . . I don't like being accountable to anyone. He looked at me; he was frightened, disappointed, hopeful, protective. You don't deserve this, but I don't think I can give you anything more.

I looked at him, incredulous.

Nazim, it was just a kiss, I said. You don't owe me an explanation. And anyway, I think I can decide for myself whether to put myself in a potentially dangerous situation and you, believe me, are the least dangerous man I have ever come across.

He tried to protest but I put a hand over his mouth.

No, listen. I like the way you smell. Don't worry for me. Soon I'll go back to the city, and you'll set sail from some port. We know how this story will end. Can you let me enjoy it anyway?

His eyes softened. He nodded and gently moved my hand from his mouth.

You like the way I smell? He asked with a hint of a smile.

Oh, shut up.

8.

Aisha was trying to get hold of your brothers but she couldn't find them. Not at the addresses you had given her in case of emergency, nor the ones in your old address book. You had learned to write from right to left, so you held your wrist in a way that stopped you from smudging the fresh ink. You had elegant handwriting, straight and long. You were slow, but you liked to write.

I know this about you because I have your notebooks of recipes and some of your letters, written in an alphabet that is unknown and inaccessible to me.

They don't exist, Berta whispered as she washed the dishes, seeing us hunched over the table googling names that we had heard a couple of times in fleeting conversations, names that could have belonged to anyone. We looked for places we'd never seen, followed the scent of rumors and ancient anecdotes. We wanted you to have your people close at the final goodbye—but who were your people, Papà? Was it just us? Where were the others?

We sent letters to all of them, even the ones who were probably no longer alive, or had never been. We sent letters chasing your past. Where is Boubakar now? I asked Berta. What about Idris? She looked at me bewildered as to what I was talking about. What are memories, if not secret stories?

In the meantime, there were new people at the bar, because the number of boats arriving had increased. People said the town was becoming the new Lampedusa, that hundreds of them were coming, mostly from Tunisia, which was going through a horrifying economic crisis, and from central Africa, where there hadn't been any water for years by this point.

Nazim was working non-stop at the reception center, mostly with unaccompanied minors, who were often no longer minors but came without documents and said they were seventeen so they could plead for a warm place to sleep. Many of them had been to high school or technical college and they often knew French or English. The older ones, however, were less educated and more angry, because the journey there had entailed a violent uprooting. Then there were the women, younger women and older women. They weren't afraid. If they had been, there was nothing that could have consoled them.

The town, in spite of itself, embraced everyone. Sometimes agreeably, other times not, but people were rarely refused, because the town had respect for poverty and desperation, and, above all else, for the sea and its laws. It opened itself to the new arrivals even when it felt invaded, and the discontent was put to one side for now. Those who could lent a hand; the rest looked the other way.

One Christmas, I went to India with Liz and some of her other friends, to crown a spiritual journey that began with downloading a meditation app and ended with the reading of *Eat Pray Love*.

Liz was different when travelling. I caught a glimpse of some of the cracks that momentarily unveiled who she really was, something that at the time made her more accessible and sympathetic. I suspected she didn't really like travelling, but that it was one of those things she felt she had to do for credibility. She travelled with a backpack, of course, but the crumpled clothes clearly vexed her: I saw her jaw tighten as she carefully laid out her sleeping bag on the single-use sheet of the boutique hostel where we had booked a whole room so we wouldn't have to share with strangers. I was terrified of the cockroaches, and I admired the austere efforts Liz made to pretend to not notice them. There was nothing in nature that bothered her, of course, but I couldn't help noticing how her shoulders relaxed when I finally found the courage to kill the roach with a decisive blow of my flip-flop. Perhaps that's what I was there for.

Liz didn't trust the little plastic bottles of water from the supermarket and for days drank only Coke Zero, which was safer than the water in the kinds of countries she liked to call *the developing world*. She took a lot of photos of places and of herself—few of other people. She preferred dramatic natural landscapes—waterfalls, deserted beaches, temples in mountains surrounded by fog—to crowded and dirty streets, monks surrounded by animals and motorbikes and filth. Once the trip was over and from the safety of her armchair, she liked to update the huge number of countries she had visited on her social media profiles. Globetrotter. Adventurer. Wanderlust. 35+ countries visited. And then the avocado emoji.

I wonder now why I ran so far away—what I was running from, and at Christmas—rather than coming home to my sister and Berta and you, who were still alive and perhaps expecting me without having the courage to call me, to say *come back*. I imagined our old Christmas tree with the golden baubles, and the cous-cous you used to make for lunch on the 25th when you invited everyone to the bar to celebrate the day you called the holiday of peace. I looked around me and thought I didn't deserve beauty, because I evidently didn't understand it, didn't know how to recognize it or accept it inside myself.

How stupid I was, Papà, and how stupid you were for never calling me.

Aisha went to the reception center in the morning and came back to the bar around four. She was tired and beautiful, her black eyes glowing. She looked happy, and I asked her why. She shrugged and said she felt useful.

The following week was the feast day of the town's patron saint. The volunteers at the reception center were organizing various activities for it, with the help of the scouts: games for the little ones, music, stilts, a fire eater, and a long table that would seat everyone in the Piazza del Duomo. The whole town would participate in the event: there were those who would cook, those who would have stalls selling caramelized almonds and frittole, and then there was pottery and embroidery by people who came down from the mountains especially for the event. People played, smoked, watched. For this one evening the migrants would join in with the celebrations, would dance the tarantella and play tag. They would have a good time and might even end up on the national news.

And then everyone can sleep soundly, I said. I was envious of how Aisha moved so securely in that complex world, and maybe I wanted to be scathing, to make her feel naïve. Her gratuitous altruism made me feel bad.

Are you feeling selfish? She asked, laughing. She knew me too well.

I felt selfish, but I just couldn't make myself go to the reception center. I looked at myself in the mirror and I was ugly. Not physically, but morally.

Listen, I said, as a thought crossed my mind. If you could really choose, what would you want to do?

She thought about it for a long time.

If it weren't for the bar and Berta and Nonna and Papà's ashes under the bed? She asked, staring at a random point on the ceiling. I noticed that I was not included in her list of responsibilities. I think I would like to study languages, she answered slowly. She was trying to imagine a reality that had never been on the table. Maybe become an interpreter, or something like that. I know Arabic and English but I would like to learn French. I would like to travel more. Go on missions with the Red Cross. And maybe get a place of my own, where I could be alone, or finally find someone to share my bed with, someone who isn't you. Stuff like that.

She stopped, embarrassed. She seemed to be ashamed that her dreams weren't bigger. I thought everything she wanted was perfectly realizable if only she had someone she could depend upon, who would help carry the things she had been holding up more or less by herself that whole time.

If I stayed, I said a bit uncertainly, if I stayed to look after the bar for a bit, you could enroll at the university. Then, I don't know, we could train someone trustworthy, like Mahdi, to look after the bar and you could be here just part-time and for the rest of the time you could do the things you want to do. It isn't impossible, you know?

Aisha looked at me, speechless, then she smiled. Nothing has ever been impossible for you. It's the thing I most admire: you want something and you get it. I would like to have the same determination.

It's a shame I hardly ever know what I really want, I mumbled. Compliments always made me uneasy.

Nobody taught us to ask ourselves what we really want, Aisha said, only what we should want. We've never felt safe enough to take risks, I mean real risks, for our dreams.

I looked up at her and felt foolish.

What are you thinking about? She asked, noticing my embarrassment.

Nothing, it's bullshit.

Oh, I hate it when you do that. Tell me what you're thinking about! It'll drive me crazy if I don't know, I'll think about nothing else all day. She grabbed my arm and pulled at it playfully.

I was hesitant, but I forced myself to say the words: Couldn't we be each other's safety net?

Her grip on my arm softened, I couldn't look at her face but I felt the warmth of her hand on my skin.

That sounds like a great idea, she responded. Her voice was warm and soft.

9.

We planned the funeral for the end of October. It was more a commemoration than a real funeral. We convinced the imam to celebrate the strange rite you had come up with after speaking at length of the many yous that we knew. It was a long and painful process but it was also beautiful. Berta hadn't wanted anything to do with it, so Aisha, the guys at the bar, and I pulled out our most meaningful memories of you, which were all so different. Aisha seemed jealous of our secret rituals at the bar, of the stories you told me that she didn't know. I was jealous of the language the two of you shared, of the prayers and Ramadan and the faith that united you. We had always felt we were in competition for your attention, but you had given each of us a different side of you—me the rascal and her the saint. Were they both true, or both false? We couldn't know.

The imam was a gentle and patient old man who had lived in the town for many years and had visited the bar on occasion. The two of you argued because you didn't go to the mosque, you drank, and sometimes you turned your back on your god; but deep down you respected one another because both of you were here to give your brothers something fundamental: a social life and a spiritual life. When word of your death spread in the town, he started coming to the bar more often, talking to the guys that were there, taking care of them. Not to substitute you, but to fill the void within each of them that your absence had created.

* * *

We would scatter your ashes from a little boat, in the sea that separated you from home, or perhaps was more home than anywhere else. The sea in which you had learned to swim—because the ocean scared you and you never put your head under the water. To the sea that had given you everything and taken it too, we would give all that remained of you.

Every day I went running and every day I found Nazim waiting for me at the end of the beach. As he walked me home we spoke of everything, and neither of us tried to appear as something we weren't, safe in the knowledge that there was no future for us. I would leave, and he would also leave, so there was no need to protect ourselves. We talked a lot about our mothers and you and Aisha and the boys he looked after, the boys who said mean things, who secretly sold drugs and secretly cried, who had scabies and rabies, who couldn't hold a fork in their hands because they had lost one finger, sometimes two. Boys with empty eyes, who would never get better, yet they were alive. We talked about them and about ourselves.

Nazim regularly asked me to go with him to the center, but I always said no, as if I were allergic to the pain of others, accustomed as I was to concentrating only on my own. I thought that if I'd gone into that building and seen all the suffering it contained, had seen Nazim and Aisha at work, their generosity, if I had been a witness to that tenderness, then everything—my city, my room, the objects that surrounded me, my sarcasm, my walls—everything would crumble, and of the old me nothing would remain, because I hadn't known how to build anything true.

The evening before the commemoration, I invited him to our house for dinner. We had all started drinking and smoking very early to numb ourselves, and Nazim ended up doing the cooking. He was so sweet with Berta—a sweetness that moved me—which Berta leaned into, the perfect victim, with an almost lascivious urgency that made me uncomfortable. If in the weeks leading up to it I had started to see an opening between us, that scene brought back to the surface all the anger I had pretended to have forgotten.

Stop it, I hissed at her. You're acting like a sick child. I stared at her with harsh eyes as she innocently braided her hair.

Why are you always so mean?, she pouted. Why is a stranger being kinder than you?

Because he doesn't know you, I responded.

Aisha moved toward me like a shadow; Nazim shot me a calm warning look. I knew they were ready to stop me, but I wasn't sure which of us they were trying to protect.

But it was Nonna who surprised me. Don't provoke her, Mina. She's fifteen again. She's convinced she's the only person who has suffered in this life. She spoke with a coldness that a mother should never have toward her daughter. I thought about how Berta's meanness was probably hereditary. Maybe I shouldn't have children, I thought.

Berta ignored her mother as if she was just a voice in her head. For a split second her face changed, then she went back to fiddling with her hair. Who knows what these two had done to each other, living under the same roof for all those years. What cruel match they had been playing, held tightly in the yoke of family, forced to look after one another, to do the things one has to do because they're right, enclosed in roles that strangled them.

Tomorrow is my husband's funeral, said Berta in a voice that was breaking. She stuffed a fistful of hair into the pocket of her nightgown. Am I allowed to suffer, mamma? Can I? Or is it too much of a bother for you, because emotions are reserved for those who have won a war?

Everyone has a right to experience their own emotions, Nazim intervened, conciliatory. Aisha shushed him with a hand gesture and he didn't dare continue. He turned around to do the dishes and hid behind the noise of the water.

Berta slammed her wine glass on the table and stretched her arms out exclaiming: Ah, thank you! At least someone has given me permission. Have you had any luck with that one? She wouldn't cry unless you cut one of her arms off. She's exactly like her grandmother. I don't know what I did wrong with her.

She was talking about me.

I cleared my throat, impassive. Everything and nothing, Berta. Maybe you needed to be there to do something wrong.

But Berta had withdrawn back into her own world and didn't reply. What is it, *mamma*? Is it not true? Tell me it's not true. Do you remember a single carnival costume? Do you remember an essay, a school trip, a play, a fucking note in my diary? Do you remember me? How I had my hair? Papà cut it, with a bowl, and combed out the lice, because you were too tired. Do you remember that, mamma? Do you remember this scar, from when I fell off my bike? Do you remember? Do you remember these? I showed her the marks on my arms, almost completely faded now. I didn't look at Nazim, I didn't look at Aisha, I looked only at her, her eyes fixed on my skin. No, you don't remember because you weren't at the hospital, because you had to rest, because you had a headache, because you were sick . . .

I heard my voice quake. It was about to happen.

I just wanted you to love me, I said. And I don't know why you don't.

She cried too, without words because there were no words to say.

Berta whispered something and stood up, stumbling, her thin hands wrapped tightly around her glass. There was the sound of something breaking, then blood. Shards everywhere.

I saw Aisha lurch toward her, and for a moment I thought of pushing her away, over the table, of pushing her face into the broken glass, because she would always choose Berta, not me. But Nazim wrapped an arm around my waist and whispered that I was strong, while she was very, very fragile.

It's not fair, I said between sobs, it's not fair. I don't want to be strong.

Being fragile seemed like a privilege that only Berta was allowed. Aisha looked at me as if to say "I'm not on her side," then took Berta by one arm and led her to bed. Nazim and I started cleaning up, while Nonna watched us in silence. She too seemed to have lost the detachment that always set her apart. It's my fault, Mina, I'm sorry. I never managed to . . . She was so fussy and so sickly. Always so sad. I couldn't handle her . . . When your father came onto the scene I dropped her onto his shoulders like a dead weight. I'm sorry. All that she has done to you she learned from me. She covered her face with her hands.

I didn't say anything, irritated because she was indirectly justifying Berta's behavior. I didn't want to forgive her.

We met again on the swing in the garden, Nazim, Aisha, and I, to pass around the last spliff and wait until the day broke. I couldn't stop crying: whatever they said, whatever they were talking about, I just kept dripping like a broken faucet.

If you go on like this you'll have no tears left tomorrow and everyone will think you're heartless, Aisha said as she rubbed my back. And anyway, she went on, I don't want to diminish what we went through—I was there too, I know. But I'm surprised that all of your resentment is directed at her. Berta did what she had to do to survive. Why are you taking it out on her and not on Papà? Is it just because she's the mother and therefore she has to exist to love us and tend to us? To love and tend to us, daughters she probably never wanted? Meanwhile

Omar was a saint because . . . because he was such a distant and elusive man that you could easily idealize him? I think I'm angrier with him than I am with Berta. Where was Omar when all that shit happened?

Hearing her speak in this way shook me, I felt a knot melting in my throat.

He came to see me in the city once, I said. I had been away a few months. He appeared out of nowhere at the place I was working. I couldn't believe it—he hadn't warned me, hadn't phoned . . . He turned up and asked if I wanted to go for a walk. Not knowing how to answer, I said I had to work. I didn't understand what his presence there meant. He looked at me as if he had come to pick me up from school. He was so out of place and at the same time, I don't know, it was so obvious that he was there. He sat down and waited for hours for my shift to finish. Then we went for a walk in a park in the center of the city. At dinner he told me the usual stories, and I told him some of my own, real and made-up. He always looked the wrong way when we crossed the road; it was me guiding him, protecting him. He made me feel so proud—showing him the places I knew, how I could move around such a big city, how naturally I used a credit card or navigated the tube.

I sniffed.

We smoked a cigarette outside his hotel, one between the two of us, in silence. Then he hugged me and put some money in my jacket pocket. He asked if I was O.K.. I told him I was. And that was it.

We sat for a moment in silence.

I think it was one of the best days of my life, I said.

Aisha looked confused. You never told me that, she said. Her tone wasn't accusatory, just surprised. I shrugged: I was so jealous of the time you had with him that I couldn't have.

That you didn't want to have, Aisha corrected me. Sometimes I wonder whether that's the reason you left. It wasn't just an image of yourself you were building, but also of him, so you wouldn't have to face who he really was.

And who really was he?

Aisha sunk her head into her neck but didn't avert her eyes from mine.

He was a man, she said.

10.

The day of the ceremony ended up being a completely normal day.

We had rented a boat, which seven of us went on: me, Aisha, Berta, Nonna, Magda, the imam, and the fisherman who had rented it to us. Aisha was wearing a black djellaba with a beautiful lace hijab: it surprised me how the Arab and the Southern Italian converged in her—the veil, the black robes, the tear-streaked face.

It occurred to me how close we were getting to resembling a real family, and how you had missed it by a hair's breadth. In truth, it was your death that united us, that turned us into the pillars of a quake-stricken house, standing stubbornly erect, remaining a refuge for the hopeless cases who had nowhere else to go. We were fatherless, all the women on that boat. We had survived bad love, disappointment, grief, solitude, and each of us had sacrificed everything we could do without just to make it through.

Berta, drugged up as usual, refused to wear the black dress we had bought her and insisted on dressing like she did for your wedding: a yellow tulle skirt, a cream blouse with bat sleeves, enormous round glasses with orange lenses, and flowers in her hair.

I softened at the thought that the young girl who had married a foreigner, and who everyone pointed at because there was something not quite right about her, was my mother, and before that, a woman. Living, for her, was a daily battle that she struggled through, but despite everything she was still there, and I admitted, in my heart, that I was grateful for that. Her daughters had been the price she paid to remain alive, but whatever I did, wherever I went, whoever I was, I had come from her, from that small defenseless body. Maybe I'd never forgive her, but I knew that I would carry on loving her. There was no other way.

The imam and Aisha uttered their secret formulas. I felt like laughing, it was all so funny: us five sitting like sardines in the bright blue boat, Berta dressed as a bride, Magda mumbling prayers in Polish, Nonna, so afraid of big emotions, feeling awkward. And then me, who had been telling myself stories about you my whole life, the stories I wanted to hear. I still didn't know who you were.

Papà, I'm scared of who I'll become in this world with no you. Who have I become over the years throughout which I pushed you far away, erased you, denied you, throughout which I hid where you couldn't see me, reach me, touch me?

Idris's Walkman, the way Zahra rubbed her swollen belly, the smell in the bar of mint and hashish, the running shoes Malik bought you with his first paycheck, jidda's hands—did I already say that?—and the price of flour, the hunger, the sounds of Derb Sultan, the flabby bodies of the old people in the fog of the hammam, skin wrinkly from the steam, from time, the blinding, bewildering colors of the market, women distractedly adjusting their hijabs, walking, chatting, and you following them with your eyes, like ghosts. As a boy, with jidda, you used to be scared you'd get lost and she wouldn't look back to find you, lost one son lost them all, the dogs that nearly took your leg off, the time you tried to steal apples from the neighbor's garden, the guy that sold odd shoes on the street corner, for people who only had one foot, the witches that read your tea leaves, the howling of the wolves in the distance from one of your great aunts' houses at the edge of the desert, lying on the roof with the stars so close it felt like they were falling down, the frightening sound of the waves in Melilla, when the current pulled you out and you were afraid of dying, when you ran from the police and you were afraid of dying, when you woke in the middle of the night and you were afraid of dying, there was a bullet hole in the living room window, you watched it, Boubakar grumbled in his sleep. A tear, like ripped fabric, but inside, beneath your sternum. It made you feel like you were and weren't there, in that moment when you dreamed of elsewhere. A restlessness, like a spirit, which lay on your chest at night as you thought of the day you would leave, as you thought about how life would be away from home, that home would be what you called another place, another bed, other walls. You wanted it, you wanted it, you wanted it, you told yourself, I told myself, because you were—you had to be—special to exist.

Did I make you up, Papà?

Me on the surface of the water, you under the sea, I saw you as a little boy, lanky and intelligent. No. Tall and strong, kind, nice. No. A boy with a snotty nose, crying. Was it you? Were you the teenager with the big hands, too big to hold a flower? The hungry, angry lad whose chest sometimes hurt, who didn't know what ambition was but wanted to feel safer? Was it you? Or was it always, always just me?

I want to join you down under the sea to ask you, but you're not there. You're not anywhere.

Aisha's body is warm and real next to mine, my thigh brushing hers. She passes me the box with your ashes in it, I hold it between my knees. I take a handful and immerse my fist in the water, then open it to let you go. The sea swallows you. I take another fistful, plunge my arm in up to my elbow. I don't want the wind to take you away. I want to see you swim, you who were always afraid of the water. Or so I thought. I rest my chin on the wooden side of the boat and observe you as you fall. Your body doesn't float, but your memory does.

I pulled myself together only when the boat started to violently rock from side to side and I heard shouts and a deep-sounding splash. Without even turning around, I knew that Berta had gotten undressed and thrown herself into the water, a white cloud in the dark blue.

The fisherman and the imam looked away while we, half crying, half laughing, watched her little breasts poke through the surface of the water as she played dead.

Ciao amore! Ciao amore, ciao! She repeated kissing the water, letting it run into her mouth, spitting it out. Ciao amore! Ciao amore, ciao amore, ciao. She held onto the edge of the boat and smiled: It was our song, she said, before letting herself plunge in again. Every time she disappeared under the water I felt Aisha's whole body tense up in panic. But she always came back to the surface.

What version of you did Berta love? Which of us knew the true you?

Either way, we loved you, Papà.

Mamma! I called out, and she came to me. She looked happy. I leaned over, my elbows on the edge of the boat and, in a confused instinct for self-preservation, I asked her the only thing that mattered.

Oh, Mina, she replied taking my face between her wet hands. So much, always. Badly and always. Without knowing what it means, but so much, so much!

I nodded, and withdrew. She started to swim toward the shore.

The ceremony was finished.

Everyone was at the bar that afternoon. All the faces that had become surprisingly familiar, and others, who I might have recognized from memories that weren't mine. Only a few weeks had passed, but that was the first time I realized I was inside that world, that it had stitched itself onto me like a new skin. Without anything outside of me changing, without cutting my hair or taking peyote—I had become who I am.

Mahdi hugged me with his thin arms and told me he had just made the best cous-cous of his life because you had guided him every step of the way. There was a time when I would have scoffed at such a statement, but in those days I saw you appear and disappear everywhere.

Nonna, without batting an eyelid, sat down in the middle of the guys from the reception center and made them each tell her their story. She spoke a self-taught, chopped-up French, learnt during a period of studying and intellectual curiosity before life pressed her into the vise of survival.

Berta hadn't set foot in the bar for years. It suddenly occurred to me that this was the first time she had left the house since I came back. She stood in the doorway like a small, frightened animal, frozen, ready to fight or flee. She had gone home to get changed and was wearing layer upon layer of bright colors. In that moment I thought she was the bravest woman I had ever met, for the dignity with which she held herself up, the strength to not surrender to grief. She looked around in silence, her eyes wide, her blond hair tied in two braids that made her look even younger and more fragile. It was Nazim who went over to her first. I observed him from afar, my heart tranquil, and I loved him. I loved him when he took her by the hand, introduced her to his friends, then helped her sit down in a corner from which she could see everything without being the center of attention. I loved him when he stopped to talk to her without it seeming like he was being kind because he had to be.

Someone arrived with drums and tambourines and everyone sang the Berber songs of your people. A woman I didn't know taught me to trill my tongue, wailing, and in that outpouring of joy and pain I felt a relief I hadn't felt for years. I could shout without disturbing anyone, I could cry without apologizing. I could dance, eat, feel my body vibrating in unison with the bodies of everyone else.

Berta took off one of the scarves she was wearing, tied it around her waist, and started to beat her feet and rock her hips and bend her knees and she laughed, laughed and lifted up her arms, maybe to you, maybe to herself. Would a time come, I wondered, when, in her solitude, she would be reborn? Would she ever know whether spending all that time in your shadow had saved her, or whether you had held one another in a trap?

Aisha cried, she couldn't do anything else. I tried not to look at her because seeing her crying destabilized me. She was free.

You were freeing us all.

Nazim found me outside on the terrace. I had my back to the party and I was looking at the sea.

There's something I didn't tell you.

Mmhm?

The Red Cross called me. There's a mission starting next month.

I turned to face him, surprised. You're leaving?

He shrugged and looked at me sideways. Do you want me to stay?

I shook my head with too much vigor. You won't make me stay, I said stubbornly.

Stay where? He asked with an innocently malicious smile. I'm about to leave. Then, with a timid voice that I had never heard him use before, he whispered: I'm in love with you.

You don't even know me, I said, unconvinced.

We fall in love because we don't know one another, he replied. And once we know one another, we fall out of love.

He rested his chin on my head, and I pressed myself into his chest.

I couldn't look at him, and I couldn't let him go. I couldn't ask him to stay, because I didn't know if I was capable of doing the same, of bearing the boredom, the resentment, of letting myself be loved.

A few hours later, in the remnants of the party for your death, once everyone else had left, among the glasses and trays of cheese and honey, among the echoes of the voices that were still remembering you, Nazim and I made love in the darkness of the bar. That's how it happened, as we were filling up black trash bags. We had used plastic plates and cups, and for a moment I had thought that maybe you deserved better, but the dishwasher was tiny and we were used to choosing the easiest way. I had forgotten all of Liz's lessons on how to save the planet with style. We made love in the middle of leftover food and ghosts of you.

Nazim sat down in a chair, tired, and said: Come here. I was also tired, tired of pretending. It was dark outside, and the sea was talking to me. I sat on his lap, a leg on either side, and he pulled me to him, his head on my chest, my lips on his forehead. We stayed like that for a while, not speaking. He slipped his hands under my dress, I unbuttoned his shirt. He kissed my neck, then sucked my nipples, for a long time, until my legs started to shake. Then I got up confidently, even though he was looking at me, and took off his jeans. We started to rock slowly, I kept my eyes closed, seeking my pleasure, mine and only mine. When I came, I collapsed onto his chest, laughing.

This won't make me stay, I whispered as I planted little kisses on his neck, on the strong line of his jaw, on his pronounced chin.

I'm in love with you.

Stop it.

Did you want it? He asked me, his voice warm and firm.

Yeah, I wanted it.

Good.

It's not so difficult, I thought.

The next day, early in the morning, Nazim woke me and told me he had to go to the port but he would be back later in the day. I decided to open the bar myself. I raised the shutters and looked around like a thief. I was always scared there, scared that someone would shoo me away.

I took my time mopping the floor and wiping down the counter. I put the tea on, the smell of mint relaxed my neck and shoulders; I felt my body going through the motions, on auto-pilot.

I was startled when the door opened. I looked at the clock and it was only just seven. In front of me stood an old, sad man. He scared me because he seemed to recognize me, while I had no idea who he was.

Sorry, we're not open yet, I said, swallowing my fear, we only open for lunch, there was a funeral yesterday. The man didn't seem to understand.

He said, in English, that his name was Rashid and that he was looking for Omar. He had a letter in his hand, but he didn't give it to me. I said that Omar had died, that the funeral was his. He nodded, he didn't look surprised, but his eyes filled with tears. He sat down at the bar and asked for some tea.

You hadn't told me anything about Rashid. About your friendship, about the period of time you spent together. You had told me about crossing the Strait hidden in the hold of a ship along with many other poor people, and that you had conquered Europe by running. You had told me you won races and met people who helped you; you told me that in France you met up with some old friends who had been living there for some time and who could get you into the system. But that you didn't like France, it was too snobby, too pretentious, and so you came to the south of Europe, where everything felt more like home: the decay, the dirt, and the slowness, the craftiness and the dart of intelligence in people's eyes, the hospitality and the superstition, the zest for life and the complaining. You had told me all this, always vague, because you liked telling me about when you were a boy but not what made you the man you became.

He had stopped responding to my letters, Rashid said.

He's dead. He died almost three months ago, I repeated. You would never have read Rashid's last letter. Where were the others? Had you hidden them, burnt them?

You are his, he said. And it wasn't a question.

Yes, I responded, yes, I'm his.

He took a sip of tea and nodded. It's good, he said, you've been taught well.

How did you know my father?

He smiled a smile that was sad, wrinkled, like wet paper. It's a nice story, he responded.

Part Four

1.

You were alone. For the first time in your life, you were completely alone. Curled up in a corner, you watched people as they came and went. Tangier made you shiver. There were things there you didn't understand, and you didn't know who to ask to explain them to you.

It was 1985. You had heard some stories about what Tangier had been, and maybe still was, at nighttime. More than twenty years had passed, but it continued to radiate the atmosphere of an international city. Bright and white by day, dark and orange by night; in the dirty alleyways, in the peeling plaster of the run-down buildings, somebody who wanted to dupe you, bewitch you, at every corner. City of bandits, Tangier, where every kind of trade thrived. Everything was a game, everything was pretend. People did nothing but exchange false promises.

Young men prostituted themselves at the corners of the medina, in the hotels, sold themselves for small change, coupling up with white men, poets, artists, photographers, architects who had come there especially, because the boys of Tangier were beautiful, sad, cost so little. They fucked them, they photographed them, they made them tell stories they could put in their books.

You couldn't trust anyone. You sat there, still, observing, dying from the cold, breathing salt. You knew ports and how they worked, but you didn't know that port, which served two seas and ahead, just a few strokes away, watched Europe. One day you would find a small city that split the sea in two, and you would call it home, perhaps in pretense, perhaps in surrender.

Old men, sitting outside cafés that weren't yet open, smoked kief pipes and played chess under the weak light of a streetlamp. Moroccans, Berbers, Turks, Africans, all had tired limbs and watery eyes, knotty hands and crafty, sweet, wicked smiles. It was the young men who were different. You watched as they followed men double their age, saw them contort themselves to attract attention, hungry and impatient. And you judged them in silence, coiled up like a cat between two fish stalls. You, so tall, made yourself small, invisible.

He noticed you before you noticed him, and he pretended not to. He was shorter than you but stronger and more robust, a clean face and strange honey-colored eyes that looked like liquid gold. He had thick, long hair gathered into a ponytail. With a few adjustments he could easily have passed as a woman, because he had delicate features, the bearing of a rich boy and the hands of a person who had never worked. He was completely out of place there, at dawn, in the stench of fish and vomit, in the middle of the many who were searching for a warm bed and some hashish. When your gaze finally landed on him, you thought he was one of the weak ones who had lowered himself to prostitution, had fallen so far from the pedestal he was clearly born on. You would never do that, even if your life depended on it. You still didn't have a plan, but you thought that in some way you would find a job, or pilfer what you needed to survive; you'd get by until you had enough money to pay the smugglers and get on a boat to Tarifa, and from there, try your luck, follow your destiny.

The sun was coming up now, the boys and the fog of the marina were dispersing. Soon they would notice you. You had to make your move. Pinching the wallet of some old man seemed easy enough, quick enough. Rashid, sitting at a table outside a café with a man dressed in Western clothes, around fifty, watched you through a cloud of smoke. The man grazed his lips, squeezed his thigh under the table, then got up to go and piss. You crawled silently toward him, your hand ready to grasp his wallet from his back pocket. But Rashid appeared in front of you with a smile and his arms crossed, as if he were posing.

I was just wondering what you were waiting for, he laughed in a friendly way. You always need to be moving, never stay in the same place for too long.

You tried to wriggle away sideways, but he pinned you to the wall.

Do you have any money on you? If you do you need to be careful, they'll stab you in the stomach to get it, or cut your trousers while you're sleeping. Where do you come from? You're from the south, right? You don't look like you're from here.

Leave me alone, you said with disdain, but your sharp words didn't scratch him. You were still trying to get away from him. In vain: he had very strong arms.

Yes, I'm a fag. And what? I don't do it for money like the others do. My father runs one of those new supermarkets opened by the Europeans. I have a big house in the medina, I rent rooms out. I don't have problems and I'm not looking for problems. I saw you squatting there for hours and I tell you that in this city you can't go anywhere alone. Do as you wish, but if you're dawdling about all day searching for a ship, someone will find a way to bend you over.

His voice was firm and he seemed honest. He was looking at you sympathetically, maybe you looked helpless, because you were. You glowered at one another for a moment, but in the end your muscles relaxed and he took a step back, running his hands through his now loose hair, which wasn't curly like yours, but ran over his shoulders, soft and shining. You looked at him for the first time with less frightened eyes, and he was the most beautiful man you had ever seen. Tall, sinuous, elegant structure: high cheekbones, thin, long eyebrows framed by a pair of amber glasses, fleshy lips, white teeth, bronzed skin. He must have been really successful, in a city like that. He wasn't the type to take advantage of someone like you, he didn't need to. He had a book in the pocket of his brown leather jacket, the kind you'd only ever seen in movies.

I need work, you said. I need to get to Germany, but I don't want anyone touching me.

He burst out laughing, a cavernous laugh, full of life. It's O.K., he said. What can you do?

I can split the wiring of one building and hook it up to the next without anyone noticing. I can sew, I can sing, I can run. I can speak a bit of Spanish and a bit of German. People usually like me. I can listen and I can hide.

I saw you, though.

Maybe I wanted you to see me.

He raised an eyebrow and nodded.

Your life was always defined by lucky meetings. Your biggest talent was that you could trust good people, who always wanted to help you, for some reason, you who were only good some of the time.

2.

Rashid's by-the-hour inn had a dozen rooms kept in questionable condition. Tangier was a humid city and everything—the walls of the rooms, the bodies of the people, the objects, and the thoughts—emanated confusion and nostalgia. It was a place of magic, but an obscure magic. The guests were often foreigners passing through, obsessed with that strange atmosphere: some stayed for months, some for an hour or five minutes. Others moved around in the shadows, but you saw them, used to doing the same. If a sink was leaking, they called you. If they had problems with the TV set, they called you. If they wanted to buy some weed they called you. If someone had punched someone else and things needed to be sorted out, they called you. You were discreet and quiet, and you became confidant and helper, painter and dealer, plumber and therapist, you removed the stains of blood and semen, ashes and tears, and you kept it all to yourself.

For the people back in the neighborhood, men who loved men were a quirk of nature. But those quirks of nature were the strongest, the most resilient, the most cunning. Strange and charming creatures—no more or less so than those who ate glass or breathed fire on street corners—who survived necessarily, because living required an immense effort that left nothing to chance.

Despite being a man who loved men, Rashid was different: he was rich, his fate had been written before he was born. He would inherit land, houses, and businesses that he would have to manage and make fruitful, to leave them in turn to his children. He would marry a woman from a good family, educated but with common sense, who would help him keep the books in order. He would provide work for the husbands of his sisters, so he could support them indirectly, and for their children and grandchildren. He would take care of the family—the only male in a generation of women. His mother, God rest her soul, wore herself out bringing him into the world, terrified of not being capable of giving birth to anything but girls. Of course, he too was a bit feminine, but this was never mentioned.

He had started to sell his body at the age of twelve, not because he needed to, but because he was fascinated by that world that was so inaccessible: sex, drugs, the community of white foreigners who lived without rules, who didn't marry, didn't pretend. Who self-destructed with grace and an absurd sense of purity. He who couldn't go anywhere, had found in that perdition an escape route without moving from where he was, in his prison house, font of sustenance and humiliation.

Rashid was spoilt and capricious. He loved to read and he wrote poetry that told stories of the Tangier he knew as a child, of tall men, sailors with thin arms and scars on their chests. You who had never loved to read, discovered that listening to him was like listening to music, the words rolled off his tongue with sweetness. One evening he revealed that he was planning a trip, a sort of Grand Tour of Europe. It would be his final farewell to the world before marrying and waving goodbye to the life he truly wanted.

Don't say that, you repeated, convinced that with the right mentality, joy could be found in all things. Rashid's anxiety mirrored yours when, back in the neighborhood, you did nothing but complain about the present. But since then you had learned to feel nostalgia for those moments. Just weeks after your departure, not knowing what Idris had eaten that day, whether Zahra and the baby were O.K.—unable even to think of jidda, who maybe hated you because you'd left without saying goodbye—far, far from everyone, you wondered whether, deep down, poverty wasn't better than loneliness. You envied Rashid: he wasn't free but he was at home, and maybe he could learn to love his wife and find comfort in the familiarity of places, in the gift of sitting down at one of those little tables that looked out on the little square of the medina and remember the afternoons of once upon a time, when he had sat there with this or that guy, and maybe he had witnessed an amusing scene or won a particularly difficult game of chess and felt proud, and just the memory would make him feel good. Your memories, however, were imbued with loss, they were all sad.

Rashid's plan was to set sail for Spain, hire a car, fill it with wine and hashish, and cross Andalusia, then stop in Barcelona, Marseille, Nice, Venice, Florence, Rome, following his whims. It was a romantic plan, but with money everything is possible. He talked to you about it often, and you indulged him, studying the maps, evening after evening, suggesting contacts of friends from the neighborhood who had managed to move to this or that part of Spain or France. It was a game of imagination, but maybe you were attentively studying every move to sow the seed of the idea of inviting you, involving you in his escape. Were you so manipulative? Maybe not. Maybe you had truly become friends, maybe you were missing having a brother. Maybe, for the first time, someone was looking after just you, and you liked it.

Did you realize how much he desired you? Did you know that he watched you as you walked away, stared at you at night? Did you sleep so deeply? He told me that he never touched you. That when you slept back to back, night after night, he always stayed awake, that being in contact with your skin gave him shivers all over his body. Then he went out and went home with others. He would come back in the morning and wake you up as if nothing had happened.

Not even a faint thought of your dreams of glory remained at that point, closer to a memory than a hope. Every night, at sunset, you went running along the port, and it often happened that Rashid watched you furtively from the little table at the bar where you met, in the company of other men he was pretending to court.

3.

One day Rashid told you there was going to be a race in Tangier and that he would pay your entrance fee. With the prize money you would be able to pay for your trip to Europe, he said, with a lightness in his voice.

You hesitated, you were scared—of losing or of winning, you weren't sure.

Come on, show me what you can do, he provoked. He wanted to help you be happy, at least one of you.

You didn't want him to think you were a coward, so you accepted.

Participants came from all over North Africa, and even a few from Spain and France. The prize money was appealing. You told yourself you were doing it for fun. You were lying: you were doing it for ambition.

Adrenaline filled your stomach with bile at the starting blocks. You wanted to vomit. Rashid had brought a book with him, completely uninterested in the race. You looked up in search of Boubakar and Idris. They were the ones you would have liked to impress—they who, witnesses to your greatness, would have gone home and told jidda all about it, and she would have smiled, her eyes wet. Who would you be winning for, now?

You ran with them in your head, you followed them, you saw them at the finish line. You finished third. You were given a little medal and a small amount of cash. You didn't hear the applause and, on leaving, walked past Rashid almost without seeing him. The bile had dug a hole in your stomach, a hole full of nostalgia. You were still hungry. You went straight to a pay phone and called the only number you knew.

Hello?

Jamal? It's me, Omar.

There was confusion on the other end of the line. Jamal burst out laughing and started shouting, speaking with his mouth far from the receiver. Omar, you old bastard, you're alive! Mashallah! I can't believe it. It's been weeks, man, weeks! Oh, Abou! Idris! Guess who's on the phone?

Your heart was beating in your throat. They were there, they were close, at the other end of the line.

Put them on, you said in a rush. You were sweating, you felt nervous, feverish. What were you going to say?

Hello? Idris's voice was hesitant, almost shy.

Idris.

You heard him sigh with relief, as if he had been holding his breath since you left.

You're alive.

Yes.

Where are you?

In Tangier.

You've been in Tangier all this time?

Yeah. I've found some odd jobs, I'm sorting myself out.

Mmmh. If you were just looking for odd jobs, you could've found them here.

It's different here.

Ah. You heard him mumble something, then he said, chuckling: Boubakar is crying. He's run away, I think he's gone to find maman. He's hardly eaten since you left.

The relief in Idris's voice evaporated quickly, leaving a wake of resentment in its place, maybe also envy. Too much importance given to you, who had abandoned them. If it had been he who left, would anyone have noticed?

Is the little girl O.K.?

Yes, yes, we're all O.K.. You know, the usual. No money.

I'll send you some.

Ah, so it's like that.

Of course it's like that.

He was angry, Idris. But you didn't notice. You wanted to impress him, you wanted him to know that you weren't there doing nothing, that it had been worth it, that it had been the right thing to do.

I won a race today.

Really? You came first?

No, third, but I won a prize.

Third! Ah, you're getting rusty.

The others were fast, you continued. It was a serious race, not like the ones in the neighborhood. I live in a hotel, there's a ton of drugs, a ton of strange things. I'm a handyman, I'm friends with the owner. He might take me with him to Europe.

Idris seemed indifferent to all this information. He didn't want to give you the satisfaction. Maybe just to hurt you, he talked about little Halima. Then he said he had to go and hung up.

4.

You couldn't have regrets, you had to move forward, so you competed again and again. Rashid accompanied you further and further away, on longer and longer trips. To other parts of Morocco, to Algeria, then to Spain. You rarely came first, but you always came high enough to win something, always just grazing the position that you could have got if you had really wanted it. You were distracted. You weren't sleeping well. You felt inadequate, and it had never happened to you before, to not try your very best just to avert the risk of losing. Rashid chose the races you would have a good chance in, studying the other runners in advance. He placed bets and when he won he gave you the entire winnings, which you sent home. Almost nothing else mattered to you; you longed for the phone calls to the bar in the neighborhood. You didn't think about how much Idris hated receiving your money when he would have much preferred your presence. One time he sent you a photo of Halima, and on the back it said it was from Zahra. But you recognized the handwriting, you knew it was him. Did jidda ever think of you? Maybe not. Maybe she was used to loss. Maybe all of them, one day, would go on without you, without a thought.

When, with Rashid, you took a flight for the first time, you were scared but you didn't want to admit it. You thought momentarily of Samir and you almost wanted to cry. You had done it. You were living the life you had dreamed of together, more or less. You stayed in the best hotels—not that you had become rich, but Rashid took care of everything without asking for anything in return. He observed you, and he knew, but you never talked about it. Sometimes you looked around and the new life disturbed you. You had launched yourself. The only thing you could do was go on.

Sometimes you drank, and when you drank you phoned the bar and chatted about anything and everything with the guys. You told Boubakar about this or that concert. Idris avoided you. Month after month, you kept telling him that you still weren't settled in one place, that you couldn't bring him there because you were still being supported by Rashid. Idris had never asked you again, anyway. In the evening, frustrated, you'd sometimes try to justify yourself to Rashid, telling him you weren't Idris's babysitter, he was big now, he could do what he wanted, he wasn't your responsibility.

It's not my fault if my brothers haven't been strong enough to get out of there. Everything I've got I've got because I've gone out and got it!

Do you miss them? Rashid asked once, in a sweet voice.

I definitely don't miss that shithole of a place. Look at where we are! You exclaimed opening your arms wide. You were in a bar full of smoke in the Marais, where young men touched each other under the tables. Rashid looked around, exasperated by your performances. He didn't tell you that the endgame was near, that the date had already been set. And he didn't tell you that what he was doing for you he would never do for anyone else.

This is a shithole too, Rashid said, I can barely breathe in here.

We're in Paris, you said, as if that was a sufficient defense.

Yeah, and we're on our own. We're running against time, Omar. You're running from the past, I'm running from the future. Have you truly lived a single minute, in the last few months? It looks to me like you're going forward in a state of inertia, just because you have to prove it was worth it. You're not present. You're there, all the time.

You shook your head forcefully. No, no. It's Idris, it's him making me feel guilty.

Yeah, sure.

What do you know? You don't understand. You have an easy life, you don't have to think about money, or family, or all the responsibilities I have on my shoulders.

Rashid looked up at the sky and laughed.

Oh, poor Omar, poor little wasted talent. You're truly exhilarating. I know nothing, do I? I don't know what it means to have a family that doesn't understand me? Restricted to one role, in a life I hate? Have you not tasted enough of this life to see that money changes nothing? That we're lost all the same, that we don't know where to go?

It's obvious you've never been hungry, if you think money changes nothing.

And it's obvious you've always been loved, you take it so for granted.

For granted? They're the reason I left!

No, you left for yourself, because you think you're more important than everyone else and you think your life has a higher value than everyone else's. You left because you feel special. And you are. Rashid put his hand on yours and squeezed it. Even though there was no malice in that gesture, you snatched your hand away.

You are special, Rashid went on. But not because you're in Paris or because you won a race or because you knew how to dupe a rich boy into ferrying you around. You think this life will make you happy? Every new thing already smells old, and you'll do nothing but wander, like everyone else, searching for something you'll never find. You know why you're special? Because you're special to me. And to your brothers, to your mother, to

Zahra, to Samir. You're special because we would love you even if you weren't. You think you deserve God knows what when in reality you ignore what you already have, and by the time you get the things you say you want, you'll have stopped wanting them. You'll be forever running away and will never stop. Like everyone else.

And so, what's the secret? You asked, your hands in your hair. You wanted to sound ironic, but it was a sincere question, filled with fear.

The secret, Rashid said, is to settle.

You drank more wine. You talked about other things. You went to dance. You ate warm bread, laughing, at sunrise. In the morning, Rashid took your face between his hands and rested his forehead on yours. You let him do it—you were tired, a bit sad, and mostly you just wanted to feel loved, even if you couldn't admit it.

We'll say goodbye now, he said.

What do you mean, Rashid! We still have a week before we go back, you protested, pretending not to understand. But you understood.

I've paid for another week, so you can stay. You'll be alright, won't you?

Your noses brushed.

I'm getting married, Omar. Next Saturday. Tears ran down his cheeks, he turned away to stop you from seeing him crying. At the point where he had touched you, your skin throbbed.

So what? That changes nothing.

It changes nothing for you.

But we can go back to Tangier together, I'll keep doing odd jobs, maybe go home for a bit. You'll see, marriage won't be a tragedy. You can just ignore your wife if you don't like her.

Ignore her. Rashid broke into a laugh. No, Omar. I'm not that kind of person, and you should know that. It's easier for everyone if we don't see each other for a while. And anyway, you're here, living out your dreams, you mustn't stop, you have to go on.

Why?

Because you can.

But what you said last night . . .

Forget what I said, I was drunk. You will go on and you'll build something of your own. Maybe it won't be what you imagined, but it will be your life. O.K.? Promise me.

You had lost your voice.

I've never done anything on my own.

You'll find someone else to do things with.

He walked away, leaving you there, frozen. He didn't look back, not even once.

You never saw him again.

5.

That's where Rashid's story ends. You would find someone else to do things with. That was your true talent, and that's life, at the end of the day, for everyone. I don't know what happened next. Somehow you arrived in the town. Somehow you met Berta. In some adventurous and imaginative way, I'm sure. You stopped running—why? I never asked you. Did you already know how to cook, or did you learn later? Why a bar, and why right on the beach? Did you miss home? Did you ever think of Rashid? Did you ever think of me?

Why do people go against their own dreams and their own plans? What happens to the imagination when your eyes are suddenly opened? Why did I leave, what was I looking for elsewhere? Why did I persist, night after night, and tell myself that was the life—the life I wanted? Had I found it? Did I like it?

I remember you as a happy man. Maybe you were. Amused, melancholic, energetic, curious, severe. Happy, maybe, like a man who has settled. Like everyone.

6.

I gave Aisha six months. A generous six months. She enrolled at the university, passed her first exams with passion and determination, while Mahdi and I looked after the bar. Even Berta sometimes lent us a hand.

It was going well for a while. The thought that I was sacrificing myself for love was a sweet thought that gave me comfort and a sense of moral superiority. I was reading a lot, enjoying the slow hours. I no longer felt lonely; what I was doing made sense.

But I was bored. I was a good sister now, and so? I was no longer interesting to anyone, meaning I didn't exist. In the mornings, after my run, I tossed myself into the freezing water to make myself feel alive. I was scared of mundanity, I didn't feel I had it in me to be a normal person. I would turn up at Nazim's house in the middle of the night, and the next day push him away. He wasn't resentful but he didn't want to get hurt, so he began to distance himself, to not answer my texts.

Then, one day, he walked into the bar with a backpack on his back.

I'm sorry, I said, biting my lip.

For what?

For not being the kind of person who will always be the same and will love you forever, I explained. And I prayed that he would understand, that he would see me, that I hadn't invented that silent ability of his to accept me without judgement. I'm not going to sit at the window waiting for you to come back. I'll want to know everything about you, everything, and then I'll get bored and you'll disappoint me and I'll hurt you and you won't want to come back to me. I'll begrudge you the things I've given up for you and you won't be able to forgive me for having trapped you in the responsibility of a life together, full of boring compromises that will only vaguely satisfy either of us.

Nazim seemed to ponder my words with care, not hearing them as a tantrum.

Probably, he said, his tone relaxed. People who stay together forever do all these things all the time, I think. It's life, it's normal.

I don't want to be normal.

No, of course you don't—it's too difficult, isn't it? Much easier to alienate yourself from everything and everyone, to feel that you're special and never actually live. I know that game well. But I know that I'm hiding—do you know that? You're not scared of the idea of a normal life; you're scared of the prospect that a normal life will reveal your mediocrity. But you're not mediocre, you would never be in any life. You are a coward, though.

I'm not a coward, I mumbled, not convinced. But I was, I was.

And so do what you really want, he urged. Not what makes you feel better, not what's right or will make you more interesting or is easy—do what you want.

Paralyzed by the fear that every answer I had given myself until this point would turn out to be wrong, I couldn't reply.

Nazim shook his head. I wanted to leave you something. He passed me a plastic bag. It was heavy. They're some of my books, I thought you could borrow them while I'm away. You can give them back next time we meet.

He knew he might not find me here when he returned, but he didn't say anything else.

I nodded, my lips tight. He kissed me as if he was going out shopping.

* * *

No doors were slammed when I told Aisha I was leaving. She thanked me for my help and took me to the airport with tears in her eyes. Like always, she hid her feelings to make space for mine. My boredom versus her hope, my fear versus her disappointment. I always won. Maybe she had thought that period spent together might heal the wounds of the past, make us all better.

But I didn't feel healed or better.

7.

The city hadn't changed, with its two complementary souls: a solid and recognizable architecture, inside which washed a variegated and unpredictable human tide. It was beautiful, like I remembered—just right, as clean and tidy things always are. But my edges had sharpened at the wrong corners. I had already been replaced by dozens of other immigrants ready to soften theirs to fit into the picture, just like I had done over the years. Tidy things are always right. Untidy, uncoordinated, incoherent things are not. I realized now how rigid I had become in my definitions. I looked at the city with a disenchantment that did me neither good nor harm.

Liz had suggested meeting in a new speakeasy in the neighborhood she liked to hang out in. The way in was through an old barbershop then down a narrow corridor at the end of which you had to whisper a password, which changed every month, into a bouncer's ear. It was a very exclusive place, part of one of the old City members' clubs, where you paid thousands of pounds a year for the privilege of drinking in a normal pub but surrounded by the right people. The right people was a category of humans that was specific and nebulous at once: it originally consisted of company bosses, usually white and male, but now it had branched out to include creatives of various kinds, software engineers, AI experts, acrobats, youtubers, and dungeon masters. There were still rooms into which only certain people were allowed, but this speakeasy sold itself on bringing together the most creative and *diverse* new minds of the city.

I got the tube there. There was no phone signal so, free of distractions, I spent the forty minutes furtively observing the strangers who shared my carriage. There was a lady in her fifties whose face was immersed in a small cardboard box of noodles; a group of chatty young women who carried bags from designer stores; a guy of no more than eighteen playing Candy Crush and wearing an enormous puffer jacket that made him look like the Michelin man. The jacket made fart sounds each time he moved. There were people sleeping, exhausted after a day of work, and couples making out, sharing one seat between two. A woman with fine blond hair and frog-like eyes openly stared at me, never blinking. An old, bald Black man was reading a book. I strained to see the cover; it was an essay by Susan Sontag called *Illness as Metaphor*. His shoulders were moving up and down almost imperceptibly, and I realized he was trying not to cry. I attempted to make eye contact and offer him a silent smile, but he avoided my gaze and perhaps found me imprudent for having slipped into the intimacy of his secret pain. I felt like an intruder and lowered my eyes. In that tumult of passing lives, I was stuck, no longer knowing how to be carefree.

After our long-distance altercation, Liz had sent me an email in which she dismissed our argument as "ridiculous" and proceeded to tell me all about her travels, her blog, her collaboration with Lush, and some of her thoughts on fast fashion, which, naturally, she abhorred. In my reply I apologized for not having been honest with her, again, but then went ahead and lied, again. I told her that your death and my stay back home had helped me put things into perspective, that I was ready to come back to the city with renewed awareness. I didn't talk about Aisha, about Berta, about Nonna, about Nazim, about Rashid, about anything that was true. Going back to pretending felt like sitting down, with freezing hands, by a warm fire.

Before I came back, I forced myself to call her and, with a

thread of humiliation in my voice that I knew she would adore, I asked her if I could have my room back. She was kind, as she always was, but replied that unfortunately it wasn't possible. But I was, of course, welcome to sleep on her sofa for a few days while I sorted myself out.

This immediately restored the status quo of our relationship. She wasn't there when I arrived, but she had instructed the new housemate to let me in. She was called Sun Yi, she had the same frightened look in her eyes that I once had, and Liz's hand-me-downs were tight on her like they were on me. On the sofa I found a set of clean sheets, a welcome note, and my favorite biscuits from Waitrose, the triple chocolate ones. She was so brazenly caring—so different from Aisha's brusqueness. I had often, in my head, compared the two of them: Aisha was my sister but I had chosen Liz, and now I wondered why. And would she choose me again? Would the tension that had crept so easily between us in the months I was away turn out to be irreversible, or would proximity bring us back together as if nothing had happened? I wasn't sure which I hoped for.

The next day they were waiting for me at a table in the corner, under an enormous mounted stag's head. Liz had taken the liberty of inviting Ashley and Emma, evidently to avoid the embarrassment of being alone with me.

Here's my favorite bitch! Liz exclaimed when she saw me arrive, stretching her arms out toward me without getting up. Her Instagram was peppered with captions like "my favorite darling" and "my favorite bitch." People were her favorite things.

I hugged her warmly, then waved to the other two, to highlight that she was still the most important. Mina has just got back from Italy, Liz said, as if she were talking about herself.

How wonderful!, the others exclaimed, envious of me, who had scattered you in the sea. Whereabouts in Italy?

Oh, the south. Near Sicily.

Sicily is on the Lonely Planet's list of must-visit places for next year. Apparently it's like Tuscany, but more untamed.

Don't they have the mafia there?

Don't be racist, Ash. Emma turned to me: I love Palermo. Those gritty cities fascinate me, so full of real life and real people.

I wondered which people were not real. Were they sitting around that table? Were they with us? I imagined Aisha, Nazim, and Mahdi sitting next to me, only visible to me, laughing at the unbearable superficiality of three privileged girls talking about hitchhiking and backpacking.

What did you do in Sicily, Mina?

Liz avoided my gaze, uncomfortable. Oh, I was volunteering in a reception center for migrants. Tons of boats arrive there from Libya and Tunisia, you know. They always need help.

That's *so* cool, said Ashley, squinting slightly. Then she excused herself to go to the bathroom and do a line.

In the meantime Sun Yi arrived, out of breath as she was running late. She sat down next to Liz and whispered something in her ear. Liz put an arm around her shoulders and ran a hand through her black hair. Their relationship interested me; I watched as if through a window onto the past. When the waiter came over, Liz ordered the same wine for Sun Yi as she was drinking.

I can't even imagine the experience of an immigrant arriving in Italy, said Liz turning to me. We are so far from those situations here that we don't even realize they're happening. I mean, it must be terrible for these people to have to leave their homes and come to a place where they're not even wanted, mustn't it? Here we're all, like, *aware*, but it's so interesting to think how a less developed country must deal with these kinds of problems. Like, Italy is quite racist, isn't it?

The turn of the conversation took me by surprise. The thing that took me most by surprise was the irritation her words sparked in me.

Things are not much better here, Liz. I told Nazim's story of being at Cambridge. It was the first time I had mentioned his name to someone, and the fact that that someone was Liz was strange and at the same time gratifying. She seemed uninterested, as if she wasn't really listening. This country is still running away from its own responsibilities with the slave trade and the imperialism that knocked out entire continents, I went on. People say the only problem is class, but isn't class linked to capitalism and isn't capitalism, perhaps, linked to the oppression of minorities? We always need someone who has less and wants more, so that we who already have enough can obtain even more. More money, more prestige.

Liz nodded silently, trapped between the moral need to agree with me and the irritation of letting me win. O.K., but at the end of the day at least here we've defeated the fascists, while you guys are still voting for them.

That's not exactly how . . .

And anyway, didn't you tell me that you've always felt uncomfortable there because you're mixed race?

That's a personal thing, I said.

Mina, stop it. This is a safe space, we're among friends. We support one another. This is sisterhood, right?

I had spent years following her, imitating her, envying her, listening to her talk about that generic *we* that included me only as her satellite. I preferred to orbit around her light than explore the dark void, the undefined shadow, the fear in me. Yet in that moment I was no longer sure I was part of that *we*, and I dared believe that my experiences, my opinions, my truths were as valid as hers, as worthy of coming out of the shadows, of being turned over, of being seen.

To tell the truth I didn't actually volunteer, I said, turning to Emma. My father died. I went home to work at our family's bar, because my mother is depressed and my sister couldn't manage it on her own. We have loads of debt and we have to pay the pizzo as well as the rent.

Liz turned white. Sun Yi looked at us, not quite following. Emma opened her mouth to express all the things you should express in that kind of situation, but was fortunately interrupted by Ashley: Girls, you will not believe the scene I have just witnessed! She was walking back to the table with a strangely excited face. There were two girls chatting, one was Black and the other one was white, and the white one said to the other one: Your hair is amazing! And then touched it! And then asked her if she knew any good Nigerian restaurants!!

Everyone gasped, their eyes open wide. I was watching Sun Yi, who in turn was watching Liz, who clapped her hand over her mouth, picked up her phone, and started typing frantically.

Maybe they're friends? I suggested. Something had snapped in me and it seemed I could no longer be in agreement with that *we*, not even on things that were right. All three of them looked at me incredulously.

Christ, Mina, Liz hissed. You're so Italian sometimes.

Where are they now, Ash? Emma asked, looking around.

Ashley turned and scanned the room. There she is, she whispered, the white one is at the bar.

We should say something to her, Emma mumbled.

At that point Liz got up and started walking toward the bar. She leaned over and whispered something to the barman, who immediately walked to the back of the room. Moments later a very elegant man came out, who approached the incriminated stranger with a very serious face. The two of them started to talk, their faces betraying nothing.

In the meantime, Liz had returned to our table and was enjoying the scene from afar, explaining what had happened to her followers with a richness of colorful details that were not necessarily congruent with reality.

Out of the corner of my eye I saw a girl fidgeting at a nearby table. It was obviously the Black-but-definitely-not-Nigerian victim. She was evidently uncomfortable, unsure whether to go over or not.

The white girl turned around in tears looking for her friend, who without moving from her seat beckoned her over. But the manager blocked her way, showing her the door. The bouncer was watching them carefully. Nobody else in the room had noticed what was going on.

I don't mean to be spiteful, Liz said in an affected tone, but they need to be told these things.

Emma exclaimed with watery eyes that the whole scene was absolutely tragic. Why lower yourself to hanging out with people like that? How highly do you value yourself if you surround yourself with people who don't respect you?

Have you noticed, I said slowly, following a contorted and fleeting thought, that even when you fight the battles of others you refer to them in economic terms? I mean, what is the value of a person? Ten pounds? Twenty? How is it measured, in your opinion?

I felt a strange euphoria as those *you*s slipped off my tongue. There was a moment of silence in which everyone stared at Liz, waiting. They knew it was she who had to talk, her and no one else.

I'm happy you're back, she said at last. That place was no good for you. In just a few months you've gone back to being the provincial bigot you were when I met you.

The punch was thrown before I could think about it. I had been holding it inside, maybe since the first time I saw her, with her perfect little face and organic silk robe. I punched her straight in the face, like a yokel—uncivilized, violent, irrational. Like the wild animal I was.

It created a huge commotion, but I felt suddenly still and serene. Even in that moment, between the two of us, she was the only visible one. My ears were ringing, I heard crying and shouting, but nobody stopped me when I got up slowly and left the bar.

The Black girl was sitting on the sidewalk, alone, crying.

I thought about sitting down next to her, telling her I was sorry, that I understood—but I realized that my sympathy or understanding or courage counted for nothing, and that I didn't really understand. I didn't know if she was crying about what her friend had said to her or what had happened afterward, or something else. I didn't know her name. The thing I knew was that, like me, it was she who had ended up alone and invisible. But the fact that her pain and her confusion were somehow linked to mine was irrelevant to her—that our solitudes looked similar didn't make us friends. I didn't know her, and nobody knew me. Now I could see it.

I walked home, thinking of Aisha and her little ambitions, of what it meant for her to have value. It took me nearly two hours. It was cold and dark, but I wanted to walk. I scanned the ground for scraps of paper, a drunk lying on some steps, some ugliness, some tear in that picture postcard. But in every corner that might provide shelter from the wind was some big planter or structure to protect the beauty from homeless people. The fog was coming in; I walked down dark streets in the hope I'd be attacked. A fox crossed my path without stopping to look at me.

A week later I put all my things into a few small boxes: the last six years of my life. Some I shipped, others I sold, and with the money I bought a single ticket to Tangier. I didn't say goodbye to anyone, apart from who I had been, a promising shadow in a glossy metropolis.

8.

Tangier was dusty. The air was saturated with wind, sand, and desert. There was frenzy in the streets, and a palpable anger that I saw in the boys who relentlessly tried to sell me things or be my tour guide. They asked me where I was going, again and again. At a certain point I gave in, I was exhausted, and told them I was going to such-and-such hotel. As soon as I tried to walk away, one of the boys, the shortest, pulled me by the pocket of my jeans and told me I was going in the wrong direction. I knew it wasn't true, that it was just a ploy to make me leave the main road so he could steal my wallet. I knew that's what people did because you had told me about it. If I'd let him fool me, I would no longer have been able to call myself Moroccan.

As I clumsily shook him off, I felt guilty—a quiet, completely European sense of guilt. I ignored it: I wanted to be tough as nails and I wanted to be alone. I had abandoned everything I loved, I was fatherless and countryless, the city had rejected me like a defective organ. I was becoming more and more convinced that I didn't belong to any place. Rashid's story echoed in my ears like the constant beat of a drum, or a heart.

I needed to know who you were before I could know any other thing.

Rashid opened the door of his hotel and welcomed me with an embrace. He had rings on every finger. I thought, I want to be like him. Well, not exactly like him: I wanted to be myself, but with the same determination with which he was himself.

He was even richer than he was when you met him, and much sadder. I don't think he had ever loved someone as much as he loved you. This thought consoled me: I felt, there, that the pain of having lost you was a shared experience, which brought me closer to someone rather than further away. Big tears fell down his cheeks when he looked at me, because I looked like you. I didn't cry, but he seemed to be crying for me too, and I liked that. He was still a handsome man, his skin toasted by the sun, his eyes golden and lucid. Thinking of you together stirred something in me.

We drank tea, then he took me to see the bar that was the favorite hang-out of his idol, Allen Ginsberg, but more importantly of the two of you. It was on Soco Chico, or Petit Socco, the little square. I let him tell me all about the city, about the two of you. For him Tangier was the melancholy of the day descending into the sea in the slow hours, waking up early and looking at the face of the person sleeping innocently next to him, and feeling alone, resisting the impulse to destroy another's peace out of envy or desire.

He was married to a very good and understanding woman, who let him get on with the life he wanted and in whom he confided often. She was called Amal, she had studied art and she managed their hotel to Rashid's great relief, since he had never had a head for business and always failed to collect the late charges from guests he knew didn't have the money. In many ways theirs was a successful marriage, perhaps even a happy one: they spoke sincerely, they were friends and confidants, they were deeply respectful, and they took care of one another with tenderness. Growing old together had united them like a pair of war veterans.

They had two children, whose conception was for him a sort of rape. When they were little and defenseless he found them ugly, as if he had expelled the worst parts of himself, the parts that pretended. He drank a lot, at that time, and was not a good husband. But Amal had been very patient, and for that he was grateful.

She didn't have much choice, I said instinctively, holding his gaze as it burned from under his furrowed brow.

Oh, there's always a choice, he replied pensively. I'm not a bad man, I would have let her go with half my possessions. My children live with such shameless privilege. I give them everything, but some things I have to keep for myself, to survive.

I don't understand how you can be happy in a relationship without love.

Young lady, loving someone without effort is a thing that you only do when you're twenty. Falling in love, when it happens like that, comes just as quickly as it goes, leaving you with a grief in your chest that will soon be substituted by the next one. But love is work. You learn to love people when they change, when they disappoint you, when they feel like strangers—in the worst of cases, you learn to love them even when you don't love them. Westerners have such a narcissistic idea of themselves that they think the person we choose to love has to be made for us, to be deserving of such an effort on our part. But it's not true. Nobody is special. And everybody deserves to be loved. So I say love, and don't complain.

But you love men, I protested.

I have loved one man. All the others I fell in love with fast and forgot about just as fast.

But why didn't you choose to love a man forever and grow old with him by your side?

Rashid thought about it for a minute, then shook his head. I don't know. I don't know what kind of man I would be without Amal, without my children.

But you're alone!

We're all alone.

I looked at my hands for a moment, before asking him whether you knew.

Knew what? That while he slept next to me he was my brother, my best friend, my father, my son, my husband, my lover? That I lived peacefully knowing that he was peaceful, and that every phone call, every letter, every word that passed between us connected me to who I am, and that now that he's dead, the person I was no longer exists? Yes, he knew. He pretended not to know because he didn't want to be forced to reject me. After all this time I still wonder if he pretended not to know because he didn't want to lose a friend, a refuge. He used me unscrupulously, it suited him to love me, naturally . . . But he loved me, and that was enough.

To me it sounds like you do nothing but pretend, all of you.

Rashid scratched his chin, then leaned forward, searching for my gaze and inspected me for a few seconds, intensely.

I pretend, he said, but that doesn't mean I don't tell the truth. What is real, Mina? My marriage is pretend in your eyes, but it's real for me. I love my children even if they don't know me. And I hope that they love me, and that even without knowing me they know who I am.

And who are you?

A good person, who cries too much when he drinks, tone-deaf, generous, a bit cynical. There. Do you need to know everything about me to know the important things? A few hours in my company will show you all of them, these things—the rest, in the end, doesn't count for much. My secrets are not everything.

My eyes misted up with angry tears.

What do you know about your father? Tell me.

I dried my eyes with the palms of my hands. I listened to my breath entering my stomach.

I know that he liked mint tea and playing rummy and chess, and that he liked winning. I know he was very intelligent but pretended he wasn't. He was modest, but charismatic. Everyone always liked him. He was disobedient. He loved secrets. He cooked with love and nostalgia—I think he thought about his mother a lot. He was scared of swimming but wouldn't admit it. He loved driving with the windows down. He laughed often. He never tried to stop smoking, he didn't care that it was hurting him. He got lazy every so often, and for him that was the closest thing to sadness. Sometimes Berta would sit on his lap and he would pull her to him. In those moments I thought they were really in love, but I'm not sure anymore.

I can see him, you know, I can see him in all these things.

Not wanting to cry in front of Rashid, I made to get up. He grabbed me by the arm. He had a firm grip, but it didn't hurt. He implored me to sit down again.

You're just like Omar, he whispered, you are so anxious to know yourself, to fix yourself, to make yourself anew, to like yourself. You'll miss life while you're running after it.

When I got back to the hotel, I opened one of the books of poetry Nazim had left me. It was by a woman poet called Antonella Anedda. One page was dog-eared and a verse was underlined:

It looks like pajamas and smells like llamas
and there's more: the shared towel
the armchairs side-by-side in front of the TV
insufferable mutual shortcomings
emptied out like endless shopping bags.
Plenty of legends, the overestimated sex
but not the solitude that comes next.
The rest doesn't amount to much.

And underneath, written in pencil in the child-like scrawl of a man, was a message:

If you go back, I'll go back too.

9.

Rashid wanted to come with me, but I told him it wasn't worth it, and promised him we'd meet again soon. Before going I looked deep into his sad, wise eyes and asked him, directly, a question I'd been nursing for a long time: Do you think unconditional love exists? I knew how he would respond, but I needed to hear him say it.

Conditions are fundamental, he declared in a serious tone.

I nodded and squeezed his hand.

The taxi driver was smoking and singing loudly, smiling. His front teeth were overlapping, but for some reason that detail wasn't out of place on his face, which was very handsome. He spoke to me in French; I was sorry and a bit ashamed not to understand him.

I've ordered a mint tea at the bar in the airport. Strangely, the smell doesn't awaken the usual images, I don't see you dead on the ground. Instead, everything around me feels very still. I take my phone out of my pocket.

I'm at the airport.

Oh yeah? Where are you going?

I don't know. Maybe home.

And where's home?

I can hear her smiling. I smile too. It's a strange feeling.

You'll get bored and run away again.

Probably.

And then you'll miss home and come back again.

Maybe.

And so?

I'm scared.

Of what?

Having someone to talk to when I'm bored, when I get back late, having to answer the phone when I don't want to, feeling the responsibility of being there when, I don't know, you need me. I'll be there. I'll be there for you. I'm here for you. For Nazim. For Berta . . . I think that being free is devastating, but not being free—if I give it up, who am I?

She sighs. You're my sister.

I roll my eyes. I want to say that's not enough, but all that comes out is a broken sob. That's what scares me more than anything else. I was so full of me, and yet so empty. I was filling myself up with other things and saying I am this, I am this, I am this, not that. A tangle of arrogance and solitude. I had made myself from scratch so as not to seem like anyone else, and I had ended up being nothing but the reproduction of an idea, something that I had only imagined. Is it really possible to isolate the essential kernel of who you are from those who love you, who live in you? Perhaps the idea of knowing your own truth is completely illusory; there doesn't exist a truer or more authentic part of ourselves, separate from others, immutable, hidden in the depths of our being. Maybe we exist for those who love us, and those we love exist for us, in the ways we see them, in the ways they see us.

I slurp the tea noisily, smacking my lips and I think I see you reflected in the glass, but it isn't you, it's me. Through the window I watch the planes on the runway. The sky is a vibrant blue.

Can you pick me up?

On the other end of the phone, Aisha smiles and says: Of course I can.

I take your letter out of my pocket. I've been carrying it

around with me since she gave it to me, but I was never brave enough to read beyond the first paragraph. Today feels like a brave day.

My Mina.

I'm sorry. Take care of Berta, I know it's difficult, but Aisha can't do it on her own. The bar is everything I've created in my life, apart from the two of you, and I would like you to look after it together. Maybe it will give you a way to remember me.

I've always been afraid of dying. At home in the neighborhood death came so easily that mine wasn't something to be anxious about, but rather something I was waiting for. More than anything else, I was afraid of being forgotten. Maybe that's why I told you all those stories, to make sure that my memory stuck. The truth of my life is less special and much more miserable than I led you to believe. Now I'm afraid that you'll keep the memory alive of a man who never really existed—the memory of the man I would have liked to have been, perhaps, and not who I was. But it consoles me that you have believed in the best version of me. I fear that I didn't protect you from what wounded you; it wasn't indifference, but inability. I have never known how to deal with the pain of others, I could barely recognize my own. Now that I sense the fragility of this life, I realize I was a coward. But I loved you and if you loved me too, maybe that's enough.

We were very far away from each other for a very long time. I wanted so many times to call you. To say you could come back. That we wanted you to come back. That you didn't have to prove anything to anyone, that we would be happy . . . That it hurt me to think you had run away from us or, worse, that you were finding yourself in this way, following in my footsteps. For me. Because it wasn't necessary, Habibi. I hope I have brought you home, now, even if it's too late. We'll never get back the time we've lost.

Home is a slippery word. I no longer know what I think of when I think of home, my memories merge together and I often feel I'm in both places at the same time. Who could ever have guessed I would have been so rich in my life. I spent so much time lost in thought, wondering whether the other road, the one I didn't take, would have been the better road, more right for me. I'll die without knowing, but meanwhile I lived this life and it was mine. I wish the same for you. You're never running away from something, always toward something. Run toward yourself, and toward the things that are enough for you, knowing that if those things aren't there, there will be other things. I did it, and I have lived a life full of doubts, never regretting anything, apart from perhaps the words I would have liked to say to the people I loved. In the end, that's all there is.

When you were little, at night you would look up at me from your crib with big open eyes, and I would look back at you. I think that, despite everything, we saw one another in this life, and if Allah wills, we'll meet again in the next. Inshallah.

Omar

Glossary of Arabic Terms

Adhan: the Muslim call to prayer.

Alhamdulillah: an expression similar to the Hebrew "Hallelujah," literally meaning "All praise is due to Allah."

Al-jidd: grandfather.

Ammi: uncle.

Ammiti: aunt.

Baba: dad.

Bsslama: bye.

Djellaba: traditional Moroccan tunic, worn by both men and women.

Habibi: my love.

Harira: typical Moroccan soup, made with meat, lentils, and vegetables.

Hawawashi: typical Egyptian dish: pita filled with ground and spiced meat.

Imam: the person who leads the prayer and is responsible for the mosque.

Jidda: grandmother.

Kief: light hashish-based drug.

Kofta: lamb meatballs typical of the Maghreb and the Middle East.

Mansaf: lamb cooked in a yogurt sauce and served with rice, typical of Jordan but present in the culinary traditions of North Africa.

Msemmen: flaky flatbread of a similar texture to crepes. Served for breakfast with cream cheese and honey.

PUCE: flea.
TAKTUKA: a spiced dip made from tomatoes and peppers.
ZAALUK: eggplant and tomato dip.
ZELLIJ: glazed terracotta tiles typical of the Maghreb.

About the Author

Emanuela Anechoum was born in Reggio Calabria in 1991 and lives in Rome. After completing her studies, she began working in publishing in London before relocating to Italy. Her writing has appeared in *Vice, Doppiozero,* and *Marvin Rivista. Tangerinn* is her debut novel.